CRANK

A RED RIDGE SINNERS MC PREQUEL

Edited by Pinpoint Editing

Editing and proofreading by Sisters Get Lit(erary) Author Services

Cover and Interior designed by Sammi Bee Designs

NOTE

Crank is a spin-off from our Savage Falls Sinners MC series. Chronologically, Crank occurs during the epilogue of Sever, book #4 in Savage Falls Sinners MC. You do not have to have read the series to enjoy this story.

1

QUINN

"Quinn, over here," my friend River beckons me over and I weave through the lines of people.

"Hey." I smile. "Wow, I didn't expect all these people."

"What do you expect when Chris Hemsworth has a new film out? That man is fiiine." Kat grins.

"We're glad you came." River loops her arm through mine as we move down the line. "We haven't seen you around much."

It's true.

Since my dad got injured a few weeks ago, I've been helping my mom take care of him.

"Have you spoken to Sadie Ray?" she asks me.

"She texted. They're having the best time in Colton. Apparently they've been hanging out with the team."

"I can't imagine Rhett and Dane hanging with a bunch of college football players."

"Neither can I." I chuckle.

My cousin Sadie Ray is with River's brother Rhett. She's also with his best friend, Dane, and a guy we also went to school with, Wesley. It's not conventional, but it works for them, and I've never seen her happier.

I've also never felt more alone than I do lately.

She deserves it. If anyone deserves to feel loved, it's Sadie Ray. But three guys... when I can't even find one guy to dote on me. Seems a little unfair.

I let out a weary sigh.

"Quinn?"

"I'm fine." I shoot River a weak smile.

"You know, you should hang out with us more."

"Totally. It's been nice having another girl around." Kat twirls a strand of her dark blonde hair around her finger.

"My dad..." Emotion balls in my throat. He almost died. Some days I wonder if that would have been better. Now he's bound to a wheelchair, angry at the world. He tries not to let me and Mom see it, but we do.

"We know." River snags my hand and squeezes gently. "But he's alive, Quinn."

"Try telling him that," I murmur as we finally reach the front of the line. The only thing that's keeping him going right now is that the Red Ridge Sinners need him to help rebuild their club after a rogue member almost burned it to the ground.

Kat orders our tickets, courtesy of her cousin Crank.

Killian Crankton.

The less said about him the better.

Kat might be sunshine and smiles but her cousin is something else entirely, and one of the reasons I try to avoid the Red Ridge compound as much as possible.

Last month, the Savage Falls Sinners patched over the Red Ridge Reapers. Crank is their new VP while Sadie Ray's boyfriend Dane is Prez. It's been a big change, but everyone is adjusting as best they can.

And I'm avoiding Kat's cousin like the plague.

He's older, all dominance and power. His dirty blond hair is longer on top and usually swept off his face. He's got piercings and tats and that whole dirty-talking tatted biker bad boy thing working for him.

Good thing I have zero attraction to bikers. Because if anyone could turn my eye, it would be a guy like Crank.

Shaking those ridiculous thoughts out of my head, I follow the girls to the concession stand.

"You want to share some popcorn?" Kat asks me, and I nod.

A quick glance around tells me I don't know anyone here. It's the movie theatre in Red Ridge. If we'd have been at the movie theatre in Savage Falls it would have been a different story. Everyone who's anyone knows me. Quinn Renshaw, the girl who lives with one foot planted in the world of the Savage Falls Sinners MC and one foot planted in high school life. It's not always easy, being two people. Sometimes I wish I was more like Sadie Ray, able to embrace club life and everything that goes with it. But I've always wanted... more.

I want to be swept off my feet by a guy, romanced and adored. There isn't much romance to be found in the club. It's all rough and ready and the guys treat their women like possessions, not equals.

"Quinn?"

"Sorry, what?" I blink at River who's watching me with a strange expression.

"I asked if you wanted a soda."

"I'm okay thanks."

They collect our order and River lingers close by. "Are you sure you're okay? You seem... distant."

"It's just been a tough few weeks," I say.

"I know Sadie Ray is your best friend, but I'm always here, Quinn." She touches my arm gently and smiles.

"Thanks, Riv. It means a lot."

Because everything is different now. My dad is bitter and angry at the world. My mom is barely holding it together. Sadie Ray is all loved up and spends most of her time with the guys. And I'm... stuck.

I thought I had life all figured out. But it's

senior year and I feel like I don't have a freaking clue about what I want anymore.

After the film we head to Red's, Kat's favorite diner. It's quintessentially all-American with its checkered flooring and red leather booths and Formica tables with tiny jukeboxes.

I instantly love it.

"Well, well, if it isn't Kat Walker." A tall guy steps into our path, his eyes dropping down Kat's body. He peruses her slowly from head to toe, smirking when he meets her bemused gaze again.

"What do you want, Ashton?"

"Is that any way to greet your friend?"

"Friend? Ha!" She snorts. "Last time I checked, friends don't stab each other in the back."

"Baby," he reaches for her, running his hand up her neck, "I already told you, she meant nothing to me."

"Save it for somebody who cares, Ash." Kat bats his hand away and makes a beeline for a booth, River following after her.

"Who are you?" He turns his attention to me.

"Someone you need to walk away from," a deep voice booms from behind us.

A shiver skitters down my spine as I turn slowly only to be met with Crank's murderous gaze.

"What the fuck did I tell you about sniffing

around my cousin?" He levels Ashton with a hard look.

"Shit, man. You know we're good together. She—"

"She told you to get lost." Crank steps forward, close enough that I can feel the anger radiating from him.

I glance up at him, taking in the sharp features of his face. Strong jaw, slightly crooked pierced nose. Ink peeks out of the neckline of his black fitted t-shirt and snakes up his throat.

Heat pools in my stomach. Stupid traitorous body. There is so much wrong about this whole situation, I don't even know where to start. Number one, Crank is like old enough to be my dad. Okay, that's a stretch, but he's still older—too old. Number two, he's annoying in that cocky guy kind of way. And number three, bikers who look like he does have a reputation of getting around.

And I'm better than that.

So while I might find him attractive—and it's impossible not to notice—I one hundred percent will never ever act on it.

"Sunshine," his gruff voice makes the hairs on the back of my neck stand at attention.

"Y-yeah?" I croak, glancing up at him again.

A slow smile pulls at his mouth. "We're blocking the way."

Silently scolding myself, I mutter something

about not needing him to rescue me as I storm toward where River and Kat are watching us.

"Everything okay?" River bites her lips, a hundred questions glittering in her eyes.

"Everything's fine. What's good here?" I snatch the menu out of the holder and pretend to be reading it.

Really, I'm trying to distract myself from seeking him out.

Who the hell does he think he is acting like he has any say in who I do or do not talk to?

"Someone you need to walk away from," I mutter under my breath.

"What did you say?" Kat frowns.

"Oh look, they have my favorite." I ignore her.

"Let me guess," Crank leans over the back of our booth, wedging his annoying face in between Kat and River. "The supersize hot dog with extra sauce."

There's something about the way he says supersize and sauce that makes my cheeks burn. I shove my face into the menu to avoid looking at him. But I can't avoid his deep chuckle.

"What do you want, Kill? Go annoy someone else."

"But it's so much fun getting under your skin, Kitty Kat."

Of their own volition, my eyes peek over the top of the menu and sure enough, Crank is watching me. His brow lifts, his eyes darkening as he brazenly stares at me.

Fuck.

What is he doing?

I'm... I'm his cousin's friend. I'm Micky Renshaw's daughter. I'm also so not interested.

I glower back earning me another chuckle.

"You girls need a ride home later?"

"Seriously, Kill, you're worse than my brother." She huffs. "I think we can manage. Now shoo, you're cramping our style." Kat flicks her long silky locks over one shoulder.

He grabs her neck and wrenches her backward to drop a kiss on her hair. "I'll be cramping my fist if I find that sleazy fucker trying to—"

"It's cute that you care, cous. But I can handle the likes of Ashton. Now go. Before I order one of everything on the menu and charge it to your tab."

"If you need a ride, text me later and I'll have one of the guys swing by and get you."

"I think we've got it covered." She waves him off, but Crank lingers, his eyes flicking to mine again.

"Well if Quinn needs to get back to Savage Falls, I'd be happy to give her a ride." The word rolls off his tongue, dirty and full of promise.

Oh my God, he didn't.

Crank winks before tapping the edge of the booth and disappearing.

"How embarrassing," Kat groans, dropping her head to her arm.

"Oh, I don't know," River giggles. "I think it's cute how protective he is."

"Seriously," Kat's head whips up. "If anyone understood, I thought it would be you since Rhett is also an overbearing asshole."

"Crank is older though... he only cares."

"I swear, Quinn, you and Sadie Ray are so lucky to be only children."

"Lucky, yeah." I fake a smile. It doesn't feel very lucky. Some days, it feels downright lonely. Especially now my cousin and best friend is running around with her harem of guys.

"Anyway, the Devil's Night party," Kat changes the subject. "You're both coming, right?"

"The what now?" My brows knit.

"The Devil's Night party next weekend. Didn't Sadie tell you?" River asks, pity glistening in her eyes.

"No, she must've failed to mention it."

"I'm not sure they'll be back, but Dane gave Crank and the guys free reign to go wild. They're going to make a scare house in an old cabin and let kids drop by in the day, and then at night... well, you know what they say." Her brows waggle. "When the kids are away, the adults will play."

"You do know we're still in high school?" I give her a pointed look.

"So? It's not like we're kids anymore. Besides,

we need to hook River up with a hottie to help her get over Jax."

"Kat, I already told you, I'm not—"

"Relax, I'm just messing with you. You think I don't know what it's like to be a girl in the club? If it's not Diesel breathing down my neck, it's Killian or one of the other guys."

"Why do you call him Killian and not Crank?" The words spill out before I can stop them.

"I dunno. He's just always been Kill to me. Besides, what kind of stupid name is Crank?"

"It's his surname," River chuckles.

They launch into a debate about biker nicknames and how ridiculous some of them are. But I barely listen, my eyes tracking Crank as he sits with another Reaper—ex-Reaper now I guess since they patched over to the Sinners—at the counter. The server, a pretty blonde thing, bats her eyelashes at him, hanging on every word he says.

Something twists inside me... the icky unwelcome sensation snaking through me. He glances back as if he senses me watching, and I quickly avert my eyes, embarrassed at being caught.

Even more embarrassed that I'm jealous.

2

CRANK

The second I see the familiar car roll through the gates at the compound, I abandon the conversation I was having with Diesel and a couple of the other guys in favor of watching our visitors.

Standing in the doorway of the clubhouse, I rest my hip against the chipped paintwork and keep my eyes on the driver's door, or more specifically, the woman behind it. Oblivious to the fact that her every move is being tracked, Quinn throws her door open and slides her hot little body out.

I bite down on the inside of my cheek when her bare legs appear. It's hot out, unseasonably so for this time of year. I've never been fucking happier about it either.

She adjusts her shorts before doing me a solid and leaning back into the car, giving me a perfect view of her ass.

"She's too young for you, perv," Diesel, my younger cousin, mutters, coming to stand beside me.

I don't rip my eyes away from Quinn, but I don't need to see it myself to know he's also more than distracted by her right now. What red blooded male wouldn't be. She's hot as fuck. And so fucking off-limits it makes breaking all the rules seem that much sweeter.

"I'm just concerned about Micky."

Diesel snorts. "Sure thing, cous. Whatever you say." He slips around me and steps out onto the gravel. "If you really cared, you'd fucking help."

He takes off toward the car, calling out for Quinn as he goes. She turns to look over her shoulder, and the second her eyes lock with his, a smile lights up her face, one that I know I'll never receive if I were the one walking toward her.

I'm not entirely sure what I've done to deserve her wrath, other than openly want her, but she seems to be making it her number one mission to convince both me and herself that she's not interested.

Which is only spurring me on to prove her wrong.

Together they walk around the car, Quinn stopping to get Micky's wheelchair out and Diesel going straight to the passenger door to help the man himself.

I knew of Micky Renshaw before the Sinners

took over our compound a few weeks ago after we lost our old Prez, VP, and a few other brothers at the hand of one of our rogue members. Micky and his Prez, Ray Dalton, reputations precede them. But I don't think he ever imagined that he'd only be here in an advisory capacity since he's unable to ride again thanks to a gunshot wound that almost cost him his life.

I can see the darkness, the regrets, the longing to get back on a bike every time I look into his eyes. The Savage Falls Sinners have been his life since he was a boy, much like the Reapers has been mine. I can only imagine how it must feel to have everything ripped from beneath you in the blink of an eye.

This life is dangerous. We're all more than aware of the reality that comes with wearing a cut but it's in our blood and we're all willing to risk everything to be a part of it. And that's exactly why he's here helping both Dane, our new Prez, and me rebuild this fractured club into something great again.

Darren fucking Creed ripped through this compound like a grenade not so long ago in his quest to take over, to make it his. But he got too cocky, tried to take too much and it ended with him in some unmarked grave in no man's land, never to be missed by a soul.

The whole thing was a mess. And nothing like our old Prez deserved, God rest his soul.

Nolan Creed was a good guy. The fucking best. He's been my role model for as long as I can remember. Him and my uncle, since my own waste of space father checked out all those years ago.

He's the reason I fought for this club, and the reason I would never have allowed Darren to take the reins when he did fuck all to deserve them. As far as I was concerned, it was him or me. Thankfully, I'm still here. And unlike him, I'll never take my position for granted.

Lifting my hand, I run my fingers over my newly acquired VP patch on my equally new Red Ridge Sinners cut. I thought I'd be a Reaper for life, and only a few months ago I'd have laughed in anyone's face if they told me I'd end up being patched into the Sinners. But I know as sure as the sky above me is blue that it was the right decision.

The club would have died right along with our old Prez if we didn't change with the times and embrace our new brothers, our new Prez.

It's going to be good for this club. It's going to be good for both clubs.

After all, we want the same thing, and I figure that working together might just get us all there faster.

Quinn still hasn't noticed me watching as she wheels the chair toward her father. The second his feet appear, I take off toward them, needing to prove Diesel wrong. I didn't just come out here to watch her.

"Afternoon," I say loudly as I walk over.

Quinn's entire body tenses as the gravel crunches under my feet. She doesn't turn around, not even when I step up right behind her.

"How's it going, Micky?" I ask, pressing my hand to the small of his daughter's back while we're out of sight.

I'm playing with fire, but right now, I'm fucking desperate to get burned.

I love the chase. I'll be the first to admit that, and Quinn, fuck. She's giving me the chase of my life right now.

A smile twitches at my lips when she shudders against my touch. Fuck yeah. The prize is going to be so fucking worth it.

Trailing my fingers across the waistband of her shorts, I step up to Micky.

"I'll be better when you fucks don't have to come and help me out of my own fucking car," he grunts.

"Dad," Quinn warns softly.

"Come on, old man. Let's get you inside and a drink in your hand."

He mutters something under his breath as Diesel takes his weight, guiding him into his chair.

"Enough with the old man, kid," Micky snaps, but when I look down at him, I find the old sparkle I remember in his eyes. It's nice to see it still exists.

Diesel bats Quinn out of the way, tips Micky's chair up on its back wheels and bolts through the compound at full speed, my idiot cousin shouting something about never being too old for a good ride.

"Diesel, wait," Quinn calls, taking a step to race after them.

"I don't think so, sunshine." My fingers circle her slim wrist before she manages to escape me.

I tug gently and she's powerless but to step closer, her body heat burning into my skin as I stare down into her green eyes. She pulls her arm as if she actually thinks I'm going to take pity on her and let go.

"Don't call me that," she hisses, her lips pressed into a thin line, her eyes narrowing in frustration.

"Why not? It suits you."

"It doesn't fucking suit me," she damn near growls. "There's nothing sunny about me right now."

"Exactly. That's why it's perfect." I smile down at her as she fumes, once again trying to force her wrist out of my grip.

"You're hurting me."

"Ah, sunshine. This," I say holding up her arm. "Is the least of what I want to do to you."

Her chin drops in shock at my words, her eyes darkening.

"Just like I thought," I mutter, closing what little space there is between us. "You want me."

"What I want," she spits. "Is for you to leave me alone. I'm not interested. I'm not sure how many other ways I can tell you that."

"Your words mean nothing to me, *sunshine*."

Silence falls between us as my eyes drop to her lips, and then lower to her plaid shirt that drives me fucking insane.

"Wow," she laughs. "Does this shit actually work on the girls of Red Ridge. I mean, I know they've all got a bit of a rep, but fucking hell."

"If you've heard the gossip, then you'll know it's not my lines that keep them coming back for more..."

"Whatever. My dad is going to be wondering where I am. And I'm sure you really don't want me to repeat exactly what you just said to him? You might think I'm some prize to be won. But I'm his little girl. His princess. And no one, not even you, Killian Crankton, will be good enough for him."

This time, when she pulls her arm away, I let her go.

"Until next time, sunshine," I call out as she marches away from me. Her hips swaying from side to side and her red hair shining in the sunlight.

My fingers curl as I imagine just how soft it might be when it's twisted around them.

I don't follow her straight to the clubhouse. Instead, I swing by my room to give her a little space while I have a smoke. I want her to relax, to think that I'm not completely obsessed with the idea of breaking her down. Because the second I get her to believe, that is the moment she'll finally drop her walls and give in to what she really wants.

"You're a fucking asshole," I mutter to myself, running my hand through my hair. "She's too young for you."

But despite the fact I know it's the truth, it's not going to stop me.

I've never been one to back down from a challenge, to let go of something I want. And I'm not about to start with Quinn Renshaw. Sinners' VP's daughter or not.

I'm determined to prove to her that swearing off bikers was the wrong decision. The MC is her life just as much as it is mine, she's just too scared to embrace it.

I force myself to stay put for ten minutes. Once I've changed my shirt, I shrug my cut back on and find my way through the hallways and into the clubhouse. The second I step into the huge room, my skin tingles with awareness as her eyes land on me. It takes more effort than I anticipated to stop myself from searching the room for her, but I keep my eyes on someone else who's sitting at the bar and make a beeline for her.

"Hey, Luce. How's it going?" I ask, slipping onto the bar stool beside one of our regular club whores. It's been a while since I hooked up with her, but she's made it more than obvious in the past few months that she's more than ready for another round.

"Crank," she damn near purrs, her eyes

running over every inch of me. "Long time no...
see."

"Things have been a little crazy. But I'm more
than ready for things to get back to normal."

"Crank," Axe barks from behind the bar,
sliding a beer across the woodwork.

"Good man," I say, tipping the neck of the
bottle in his direction.

"You know," Luce drawls, lifting her fingertips
to the patch on my cut. "This looks damn good on
you, VP."

Looking down, I watch her talon of a nail trace
the letters before movement over her shoulder
catches my eye. This time I can't fight the smirk
that finds its way onto my lips as I watch Quinn
storm out of the clubhouse.

"As good as this little catch up has been," I say.
"I've got business to attend to."

Draining my beer, I turn toward where Micky,
Diesel and a couple of my brothers are. "Ready, old
man?"

He growls, his jaw popping in frustration. "It's
a good thing I like you, Crank," he mutters,
wheeling himself over to me.

"Come on, we've got business to discuss."

3

QUINN

"Hey, I didn't expect to see you here," Kat approaches me sometime later as I perch on a stool at the bar.

The Red Ridge clubhouse isn't all that different to the one in Savage Falls. There's the standard bar with a shiny chrome and metal bar running across the length, complete with stools. Then on the other side of the room is a long black leather banquette that runs along two walls. There's a pool table in the corner and an old jukebox, and a ton of club paraphernalia hanging on the walls.

"My mom asked me to give Dad a ride, so here I am." I purse my lips.

"Don't look too pleased about it," she chuckles. "At least we can keep each other company. I promised Diesel I'd study but screw that. What do you say we go outside and catch the last of the rays?" Kat nudges my shoulder.

"Sure." Anything beats sitting in here watching the club whores sit around waiting for the guys to reappear.

My eyes flick to the woman Crank was flirting with earlier. She's pretty, really damn pretty. Her long blonde curls fall over her shoulders, highlighting her ample cleavage that spills out of a skin-tight tank top. She has legs for days and curves in all the right places.

"Hey, you okay?" Kat nudges me again, and I blink over at her.

"Huh? Uh, yeah." I glance back at the woman. "Who is that?"

"Who, Lucy? She hangs around here a lot. You know how it is."

"Is she... with one of the guys?"

Kat snorts. "She wishes, they all do. Got her hooks into Crank a couple of times but he's not the settling down type of guy."

My stomach twists at her words.

"Why do you ask?"

"No reason." I shrug. "She was staring at me earlier and I wondered what her problem was." The lie rolls off my tongue.

"Yeah, she's a real bitch. Thinks because she hooked up with Crank a few times that she's his favorite or some shit."

Lovely.

"Shall we?" I motion to the door and Kat taps the counter and says, "Let's go."

But just as we reach the door, Lucy approaches. "Hey, Kitty Kat," she purrs.

"Luce."

"Who's your new little friend?"

"This is Quinn, she's Micky Renshaw's daughter. This is Lucy Drakeford, she's... around a lot."

"Oh, Kat silly, you make it sound like I'm just another club whore when we all know I'm more than that."

"Whatever you say, Luce."

She flips her blonde curls off one shoulder and smirks right at me. "I love your hair. You remind me of someone..." she clicks her fingers, "Oh my God, I know. Ginny Weasley from Harry Potter."

"I don't see it," Kat jumps to my defence.

"Sure, you do. All that red hair and cute geek thing you've got going on."

I glance down at my shorts and plaid shirt. Sure, I don't look like the women here in their skin-tight skirts and leather boots. But I like my casual, yet easy style.

Besides, it's not like I'm looking to impress anyone.

"This has been fun and all," Kat grabs my hand, yanking me toward the door, "but we have things to do. See ya."

We spill into the afternoon sun and Kat says, "Ignore her. You look nothing like Ginny Weasley.

She's just being a bitch, probably because you're higher in the club hierarchy than her."

"Trust me, I'd rather not be."

"You don't mean that."

I shrug, following her around the side of the clubhouse to the fire escape stairs. Kat starts climbing and I frown. "Uh, where are we going?"

"Come on." She glances back at me. "It's perfectly safe."

All the creaking and clanking suggests otherwise, but I follow her, wanting nothing more than to escape Lucy and her barbed words.

Kat disappears over the edge of the roof and I follow, sucking in a sharp breath when my eyes land on the setup. It's a flat roof that someone has turned into a hangout area. There's an L-shaped sectional and table, two garden loungers, and an array of chairs. There's even a firepit. It's very cool.

"Wow, this is a surprise."

"Right?" Kat grins. "It's where I come to get away from it all. The guys don't tend to come up here, but me and some of the other club kids hang out up here. And the view isn't too bad either."

She isn't wrong. The river glistens in the distance, the trees providing plenty of privacy.

"Come on," she motions to the garden loungers. Kat peels off her t-shirt and drops down onto one of the loungers. "Make yourself comfy. No doubt they'll be a while."

I sit down, leaning back and kicking up my legs. But unlike Kat, I leave my shirt on.

"So Quinn Renshaw, tell me more about yourself."

"Uh, what do you want to know?"

She glances over at me and smirks. "The good, the bad, and the ugly, of course."

"There really isn't much to tell." I shrug, realizing now how lame that sounds.

"I don't buy that for a second. I've heard some of River's stories about you and Sadie."

"My cousin is a handful."

"She must be if she needs three guys to keep her in check." Kat chuckles. "So not fair. I can't even find one guy, let alone three. What about you, got your eye on anyone?"

Crank's infuriatingly handsome face pops into my mind but I immediately force myself to think about something—*anything*—else.

"Nope, no one special."

"Oh, I know. We should totally go out. The three of us. Me, you, and River. I can get us some fake IDs from a friend so we can hit up The Deck."

"The what?"

"It's a bar on the other side of town. It has live music on the weekend. It's popular with college kids."

"Fun."

"It is. And we should definitely go."

"Yeah, maybe."

I can wear my best Ginny Weasley cute geek outfit and maybe meet my very own Harry Potter.

Ugh.

Why am I even bothered about what that bitch said? I've never cared what people think about me before, I'm not about to start now.

Except, I saw the way Crank looked at her. I saw the raw lust in his eyes. He's into that—into girls who look like her.

I doubt a guy like Crank even knows who Ginny Weasley is.

God, I'm ridiculous.

I don't even like Crank. He represents everything I despise—everything I've always promised myself I won't get involved with.

Lucy is welcome to him.

I have never been very good at lying to myself.

We lie in the sun for an hour until the last of the day's heat burns away, then we head back inside.

Of course, because the universe hates me, Lucy is all over Crank.

Kat makes a beeline for her brother while I head for my dad.

"Hey, sweetheart," he says, looping his arm around my waist. It still hurts to see him in a wheelchair. He's always been such a strong alpha male.

"Did your meeting go okay?" I ask.

"Sure did. I need to talk to a couple of the guys about overhauling some things at the shop. You good for a bit longer?"

"Sure." I smile thinly.

"That's my girl. I'll be back as soon as I can." He squeezes my hand and wheels off, leaving me alone.

I take a seat at the bar and the club prospect offers me a drink. "Soda, please."

"I'm Tank."

"Quinn."

"You're Micky's kid, right?"

"Kid?" I balk. "How old are you, prospect?"

"Nineteen, and I meant no disrespect." He dips his head in apology.

"Yo, T," Crank calls over, "don't you have something to go clean?"

Tank mutters something under his breath and shoots me a weak smile. "See you around, Quinn."

I glower over at Crank, wondering what the hell his problem is. Lucy is practically hanging off his arm.

"Hey, Ginny," she calls. "You should come join us?"

"I'm good thanks," I mutter, turning back around.

A second later, they all burst out laughing and I can't help but think I'm the brunt of the joke.

Draining my soda, I slam the can on the

counter and stand. Kat is still talking to her brother, so I decide to head back outside without a second glance back at Lucy and Crank.

They deserve each other.

The sun is sinking into the horizon, dusk falling over the compound as I walk to the far end of the building and sit out of sight on a stack of crates. Club life is a part of me, or at least, it should be. I was born and raised in the Sinners MC, but I've never truly felt at home, not in the way Sadie does. I guess it's why I try so hard to not be like them.

But now Dad needs me more than ever and I don't want to disappoint him.

Ugh.

I lie back on the crate and stare up at the sky, wondering what my cousin is doing right now. I might not want my very own bad boy biker, but I can't deny a part of me longs for what Sadie has with the guys. They would do anything for her— literally kill for her. I've never even come close to having that kind of love.

My eyes flutter closed until I sense eyes on me. Pushing up on my elbows, I look around only to find Crank standing in the shadows, watching me.

"Stalker much," I snap, sitting upright.

"Relax, *Ginny*. I just want to make sure you're okay."

"One. Don't call me that. And two. Believe it or not, I am quite capable of looking after myself. Besides, the only thing I seem to need protecting from right now," I hop down off the crate and step up to him, "are stalker bikers who need to mind their own fucking business."

Shouldering past Crank, I walk away from him, but he grabs my arm and yanks me backwards.

"What the hell," I seethe as he presses me up against the wall, caging me in with his muscular inked arms. "I swear to God, Crank. Let me go or I'll scream." And maybe I'll knee him in the balls.

"Easy, sunshine. I just want to talk." He drops his head to my neck, and I swear he smells me.

"What the hell are you doing?"

"You smell so fuckin' good."

"Ugh, gross. So gross." I try to push him away, but he leans closer, aligning every part of him with every part of me.

He's close, too close. I can't think straight with him all up in my space like this.

"Move." It comes out less of a warning and more of a breathy plea. "Right now."

He watches me, and I feel like prey caught in his predatory gaze. "Fuck," he murmurs, tearing away from me and jamming his fingers in his hair.

The urge to do the same washes over me and I thrust my hands into the pockets of my shorts.

What the hell is wrong with me?

"I'm leaving now," I say, all but running from him.

"Hey, sunshine?" he calls, giving me pause.

Keep walking.

Just keep walking.

But curiosity wins out and I glance over my shoulder and scowl at him. "What?"

A playful smirk tugs at his mouth as he leisurely runs his gaze down my body and back up again. "You know, screaming only makes it sweeter."

I don't satisfy him with an answer, hurrying away from him before he sees the flush on my cheeks.

Or hears my heart beating wildly in my chest.

4

CRANK

"Does she really just expect me to sit around here and not get involved?" Diesel mutters from where he's sitting opposite me in the clubhouse downing his beer in frustration. "She's got a fake ID and everything, and assumes that I'm just going to let it go."

His words barely register with me, I'm too busy scrolling through an image search of Ginny Weasley, trying to see the similarities that Lucy can apparently see. I had no idea who she was talking about the other day when she first called Quinn it, so I just humored her, swiftly followed by kicking her off my lap so I could follow the girl in question.

I shouldn't have done it. I knew that before I moved.

I should have accepted what Lucy quite clearly wanted from me and attempted to get my kicks with her. But I knew it wasn't going to happen. No matter how much she wiggled around on my lap, how risqué her touches got, my body, and more importantly, my head, just wasn't getting on board with her plans.

There was only one girl firmly in my mind.

Girl.

Yeah. And isn't that the fucking issue.

She's too fucking young for me. Too innocent. Too pure. Not to mention she's the Sinners ex-VP's daughter and their Prez's niece.

I can practically feel Micky and Ray's guns pointed at me for even thinking about her. But even that isn't enough to stop me.

"Crank, are you even listening to me?" Diesel complains, throwing a bottle cap at me.

"Totally. Kat. Fake ID. The Deck. She's eighteen. You were doin' that kinda shit at fourteen. Do you really expect me to sympathize here?"

"But—"

"She's your little sister, I get it, man. I wanna wrap her up in cotton too. But you can't. She'll hate you for it."

"Like she doesn't already," he mutters, knocking another cap off a bottle and tipping it to his lips. "If Ray and Micky find out she's dragging River and Quinn right along with her they'll lose their shit."

Now that gets my attention.

"She's taking who?" I ask, my attempt at casual

is failing miserably if Diesel's quirked brow is anything to go by.

"River and Quinn. The Sinners princesses."

"I know who they are," I spit, not needing him to rub salt into an already sore wound.

It's been days since Quinn was here last and I swear I've spent every second of every day trying to convince myself that I really didn't need to see her again, have her scent filling my nose, her body pressed up against mine.

Fuck. She lined up with me so fucking perfectly. If she melted into me like I craved and I lifted her leg then...

"For fuck's sake, Crank. It's like you're in a different fucking state. Do you need to get laid or something?"

"Or something," I mutter, taking a pull on my beer. "So when are they going out?" I ask, trying to appease him.

"Tonight. They're all at Mom's getting ready."

Well, shit.

"Just leave her to go wild for the night," I force out.

He stares at me, disbelief written all over his face. "You don't actually think I'm going to let that happen, do you?"

I shrug. He knows I won't. He knows I'm as protective of Kat as he is. But fuck. I need a reason to keep my ass in the compound tonight and not find myself chasing my new addiction to The Deck to get my next hit.

"She's gotta grow up and live her own life some time. Why not right now?"

"Unbelievable," he mutters, pushing from the chair and collecting up his empty bottles. "Un-fucking-believable."

I guess I shouldn't really be surprised that only three hours later, I find myself walking toward the entrance to The Deck with Diesel right beside me and a few of the other guys trailing behind.

Unlike me, they were more than up for a night out outside the walls of our compound for once. They didn't give a shit that we're basically here on an unwanted babysitting gig. They just want fresh pussy. On any other day, I'd be right there with them. But since finding Quinn in the Sinners clubhouse all those weeks ago, all my normal seems to have gone right out the fucking window.

Security let us all inside the second we walk up to them, much to the delight of everyone else who's waiting in line.

"Long time no see, bro," Weston says as I pass him.

"It's been an interesting few weeks."

"So I heard. You all Sinners now, right?"

"Yep. Never thought I'd see the day but here we are."

"I hope it all goes well for you, man."

"Same." I bump my fist to his, then he lifts the rope for me before I step into the building and leave him to do his job.

The music pounds through my body, the floor beneath me vibrating with the low bass and I can't help but feel a little excitement rush through my veins.

We descend the stairs. The majority of the crowd will be up on the deck that hangs right out over the river, but ducking against the norm, we always head for the basement where the lighting is lower, the air is thicker, and the goings on are often more than questionable.

I figure it's a safe bet because Kat would never bring the likes of Quinn and River down here. She knows the reputation of this place as much as we do. She might be all for letting out her inner wild child, but I think that might push her beyond her limits.

I follow the guys to the bar, and the second Diesel passes me a glass of what I assume is whiskey, I knock it back in one, wincing as the alcohol hits my throat, burning all the way down to my stomach.

"I'm gonna need a few more," I shout over the music.

The bartender obliges and I throw back

another two before the warmth in my belly settles my slight unease.

She's here, upstairs most likely. Drinking, dancing... grinding up against some other guy.

I don't care, I try to tell myself. But it does fuck all to help get her out of my head.

If some other motherfucker touches her, tries to hurt her...

My fists curl at my side but no one around me notices. They're all too busy getting their night started.

It hasn't always been that way. Dev would have noticed. Hell, he probably would have seen right through all my bullshit, and less than appropriate desires when it comes to Quinn Renshaw and refused to let me come here tonight.

I smile to myself thinking of my best friend. Just another unlucky motherfucker to fall at the hands of Darren Creed.

The two of us were inseparable ever since I moved to Red Ridge. We shared a love for the club, and for as long as I can remember we dreamed of one day taking over. Working side by side and moving the club onto bigger and better things.

A long, painful sigh passes my lips as I reach for another drink in the hope of drowning out the pain.

That's all this thing with Quinn is, I reassure myself. It's a distraction from everything that went down. From the images of watching that one single fucking bullet rip right through his heart.

She's a lifeline. A ray of fucking sunshine all wrapped up in a hot little sassy package that I'm desperate to unravel. She says that this life, the likes of me, aren't it for her. But I see more than she does. I see everything she refuses to accept when I look into her eyes, and I'm desperate to show her exactly what she's missing out on. Because like it or not, she's one of us. The MC runs through her blood just like it does mine. She just needs the right person to show her just how incredible it can be.

"Well, well, well, fancy seeing you here," a familiar, yet totally unwanted voice whispers in my ear.

The hairs on the back of my neck stand on end, and not in a good way, when Lucy scratches her fake nails down my bare arm.

"I'm sure it's anything but a coincidence," I mutter, shooting Diesel a look that would make others cower. That fucker though only smiles back at me.

Interfering little shit.

"Dance with me," she whispers, pressing her breasts against my arm in the hope of convincing me.

I glance over at the dancefloor. There are a couple of strobe lights illuminating the figures gyrating in the darkness. The sight doesn't make me any more likely to agree to her plan. Well, that is until a familiar flash of red hair fills my eyes.

The light is gone again in a heartbeat, making

me wonder if it was nothing more than a figment of my imagination. But my confusion is enough for Lucy to lead me toward the crowd before turning her back on me and shoving her ass against my crotch, grinding down on it in time with the music.

I barely move. I can't as my eyes frantically search the darkness for that hair. It's someone else. Someone sent to torment me further. But even knowing that doesn't stop me.

One song blurs into another, and then another.

The rest of the guys eventually join us, each finding a more than willing girl to run their hands all over as the music continues to pound around us.

Lucy has her arms over my shoulders, her lips attached to my neck as she desperately tries to stir my body to life like I know she wants, although she's failing miserably, when I finally get another look of the girl with the red hair.

I knew it wasn't my imagination.

Much like Lucy, Quinn has got her arms over a guy's shoulders, her body moving fluidly to the beat. They dance together like they know each other, like it's not their first night together.

But even watching them, I know. Something deep inside me just knows that it's her.

And as if she's aware of my attention, she spins, turning her back on the guy she's dancing with and her eyes almost immediately lock onto mine. Shock covers her face for a beat before my eyes drop to where the guy's hands are gripping her hips.

My teeth grind and my heart begins to pound in my chest before they're both plunged into darkness once more.

"That's more like it," Lucy purrs, her hand descending my stomach, clearly feeling a change in me, but I catch her hand before she gets to my belt. "Crank?"

My lips part, I'm about to tell her that I can't, that I don't want her when the light falls on Quinn again and I'm forced to watch as the guy runs his hands up her stomach and cups her breasts.

Her head falls back on his shoulder, her lips part in pleasure but her eyes are locked on mine as if she's daring me to take what I want. To rip that motherfucker away from her body and make her mine instead.

But I can't.

Can I?

5

QUINN

I can't believe he's here... with her.

Anger races through my blood as the guy I'm dancing with squeezes my breasts. It feels good, too good. But maybe that's the liquor talking. Kat made us do shots, too many. And now everything is spinning and I'm hot... and Crank is dancing with Lucy like he wants her.

God, why does he want her, of all people?

And more to the point, why do I even care?

I don't want Crank. He's old—too damn old—and he's all growly and alpha, and he's staring at me like he's ravenous.

Sweet baby Jesus.

Heat bursts in my stomach, but it's no longer from the guy touching me. It's from the guy across the dancefloor, watching me.

Stalking me.

Lucy snaps her fingers in front of his eyes and

hooks her arms around his neck, forcing him to pay attention to her.

Bitch.

"You're so fucking hot," the guy drawls, his touch clumsy and his dancing terrible. Wait until I find Kat. Her and her bright ideas. I'd been prepared for drinking and dancing, I wasn't prepared for some guy to drag me onto the dancefloor and feel me up.

What the hell am I doing?

I grab his hands and shove them away.

"Whoa there," he chuckles, snagging my wrist and spinning me around. "It's like that, is it?" His brow lifts playfully.

But I'm done playing.

I risk a glance back at Crank and sure enough, Lucy is grinding herself on him.

Asshole.

"I have to go," I rush out, trying to shuck him off.

"Go? But we're just getting started." He guides my hand to his junk and I retch a little.

"Ew, gross."

"You won't be saying that when you're on your knees with your mouth wrapped around—"

"Seriously?" I balk, suddenly feeling very sober. "Does that line actually work?"

His expression falters, embarrassment staining his cheeks. "Fucking cocktease," he spits. "I'm out of here."

"That would be a good fuckin' idea, kid," a deep voice says over my shoulder.

I don't need to glance back to know it's Crank in all his irritating glory.

"Who the fuck are you?" The guy stands a little taller.

"Someone you really don't want to piss off. Now run along. Me and Ginny have unfinished business."

"Ginny, who the hell is Ginny? I thought your name was Casey."

Crank snickers and I jab him in the stomach with my elbow.

"This has been fun and all," I say, "but I'm out of here."

Ducking between them, I melt into the crowd, needing to get away from Crank. He's too... too everything, and I don't trust myself right now to be near him.

For his benefit as well as mine.

The bar is crammed so it's not easy weaving in and out of gyrating couples and drunken groups of girls and guys. I'm almost at our table, when a guy barrels straight into me.

"Watch it, asshole," Crank booms, shoving him hard. The guy staggers back, taking one look at my protector and mutters an apology as he hurries away.

"Go away," I snap, walking straight past our table.

Kat and River are nowhere to be seen anyway. Desperately, I scan the room looking for them but it's useless. It's dark and smoky and too crowded.

"Sunshine, hold up," Crank yells from somewhere behind me but I don't stop. I can't.

The way he looked at me back there, it disarmed me.

He disarms me.

And nothing about tonight is a good combination.

I race up the stairs, leading to the entrance and hurry out onto the sidewalk. Digging my cell phone out of my purse, I text River and Kat to let them know I'm taking a cab home.

This was a bad idea.

Why the hell did I let them talk me into it?

I move down the sidewalk ready to flag down a cab. One appears seconds later, slowing down. The window lowers, and I lean in and say, "I need to get back to Savage Falls."

"No problem, hop in." Grabbing the back door handle, I pull it open, but someone yanks me back.

"What the fuck are you doing?" Crank grits out.

"Me?" I shriek. "What the hell are you doing?"

"Uh, I don't got all day," the cab driver says. "Do you want a ride or not?"

"Yes," I snap, the same time as Crank barks, "No!" He ducks his head inside and says something before slamming the door closed.

"Seriously? I need that ride, asshole." I watch the cab drive off.

"If you need a ride, it'll be with me, not some sleazy cab driver who preys on young unsuspecting girls like yourself."

"Oh, that's really rich coming from you." My eyes narrow, anger pouring off of me.

How dare he?

Crank steps up to me, lowering his head. I have to crane my neck up to look him in the eye. But I do, because fuck him and his Neanderthal ways.

"What the fuck is that supposed to mean?"

"Nothing." My lips thin as I turn away from him. "It means nothing."

"You're a fuckin' pain in my ass," he mutters and my head whips around. The smirk gracing his face tells me I stepped right into that one. "Let's go."

"Go?" I stare at him in disbelief. "I'm not going anywhere with you."

"Sure, you are. Unless you want me to go find your little friend. I'm sure he wouldn't mind helping you get home."

"Good, do it. And while you're at it, why don't you find Lucy, she sure looked happy dry humping your dick."

"You thinkin' about my dick, sunshine?" Crank crowds me back against the wall, one of his hands coming up above my head. The shadows envelop us, his body towering over mine. He makes me feel small, insignificant.

But it's more than that.

Killian Crankton terrifies me.

The way I react to him terrifies me. I've never felt such a visceral reaction to a guy before. And of course, he just has to be a heavily tatted, dirty-mouthed biker.

Fuck my life.

"You're disgusting," I seethe.

"And you're fuckin' stunning." He drops his head to the crook of my neck, breathing me in.

"No, *no!*" My palms slam into his chest. "You don't get to do this again. Me and you, never gonna happen, asshole."

"We'll see." His eyes darken. "Now let's go, sunshine, or I'll throw you over my shoulder and carry you."

"You wouldn't dare..."

He chuckles darkly. "If you think I wouldn't then you clearly don't know me very well."

I don't know you at all. I swallow the words. I have to keep some distance between us or before I know it Crank will smash through every defense I have. I can already feel him burrowing his way under the walls I've built around myself.

"What's it going to be, sunshine?"

"I'm not—"

Before I can think, Crank picks me up and flips me over his shoulder, slapping his hand on my bare ass under my dress. "Nice," he chuckles again as he gives my soft flesh a little squeeze.

Little shocks fire off around my body, and I internally groan. What the hell is wrong with me? Being manhandled like this isn't supposed to feel good. But there's something about the possessive way he holds me and stalks off down the sidewalk, slipping between two buildings that makes my heart race.

I'm clearly faulty.

Or sexually frustrated. Yeah, that must be it.

Crank drops me to my feet beside his bike. "On you go."

"Not gonna happen." I shake my head. I've only ever ridden the back of my daddy's bike, and that was enough to scare me half to death.

"You know, Lucy might be onto to something calling you Ginny Weas—"

"Fine," I snap, hating that he's used my one insecurity against me. Cautiously, I start to climb onto the back of his bike but Crank murmurs something under his breath, then in one swoop, he lifts me and deposits me on the back.

"You'll need this." He hands me his helmet.

"What will you wear?"

"Worried about me, sunshine?"

"More concerned about what will happen if you hit your head while you're riding with me on the back."

"Keep tellin' yourself that." He winks—actually winks—before manoeuvring himself onto the front.

Grabbing my hands, he wraps them tightly around his waist allowing my hands to rest against his firm abs, and yanks me forward. My thighs stretch around his big body and my chest presses tightly to his back. There isn't an iota of space between us, but Crank doesn't seem fazed by it in the least.

"You feel good wrapped around me, sunshine." He kicks the starter, and the engine rumbles to life beneath us.

"Please don't let me die," I shout over the noise, and Crank explodes with laughter.

"You're good, sweetheart," he says, taking off down the alley.

And as the balmy air whips around us, I swear I hear him murmur, "I need you alive for what I have planned."

"This isn't my house," I say the second Crank lets me off his bike.

"Uh, weird." He shrugs, taking off toward the small wooden cabin overlooking the lake.

My heart is still in my throat, adrenaline coursing through my body. I'd be lying if I said it wasn't a rush riding on the back of Crank's bike, but I'll never admit that to him.

"Where the hell are you going?" I march after him. "I thought you were taking me home."

"The night's still young, sunshine. Besides, you're still drunk, you need to sober up, and I know just the thing."

"I am not... whoa." My head spins and I reach out, grasping at thin air to try and steady myself.

"Easy there." Crank is by my side in a second, wrapping one of his arms around my waist. "You need to soak up the liquor."

"So you brought me to the lake? That's not creepy at all."

"Do you ever shut up?" He quirks a brow.

"I shut up. Unlike you, who loves the sound of his own voice."

"Nice comeback." His lips twist in a smug smile.

"Whatever." I avert my gaze. He makes me crazy. But he isn't wrong, all of a sudden, I don't feel so good.

"The Shack has the best damn dirty fries in the whole of Red Ridge."

"The Shack," I say, pulling out of his hold. When he touches me, I feel unnerved, like I might try and climb him like a tree and beg him to touch me.

And that isn't an option, like ever.

"Yeah, I know the owner, Jerry. He's a solid guy. Come on." He grabs my hands and tugs me toward the nondescript cabin.

"There isn't even a sign."

"He doesn't need one. Everyone knows about this place. It's that damn good."

Crank opens the door and I'm surprised when he motions for me to enter ahead of him. "I didn't have you down as a gentleman," I sass.

He leans down and whispers, "I didn't have you down as a cocktease, but here we are." With a deep chuckle he moves past me and calls out for Jerry.

While I stand there wondering what the hell I've gotten myself into.

6

CRANK

We stand together in the entrance to The Shack as I run my eyes over the busy diner looking for Jerry. Quinn's body burns against the side of mine, making my need to take her around the back of the building and deep into the forest that surrounds this lake almost too much to bear.

I should've just taken her home, but the only thing worse than Micky catching me with his precious daughter on the back of my bike would be her being drunk off her ass. I've got a rep, one that I'm sure he knows all about. And while I might not have the best of intentions where Quinn is concerned, I don't want everyone, including her old man, knowing about it.

I just need to get her out of my system and then my life can continue as it usually does. Without the constant thoughts in my head that involve her body, her red hair, how her full lips might look wrapped around...

My cock jerks in my pants and I slam down that line of thought.

Sober her up and take her home. That's all this is.

"Killian," Jerry booms across the large space when he finally emerges from the kitchen. A wide smile pulls at his lips, one that I'm sure matches my own as he approaches. "Long time no see, my boy. I was starting to think I'd done something wrong," he jokes.

"Nah, never. It's just been a mad time, I'm sure you've heard."

"Sure have. Turn around," he instructs, and I've little choice but to do as he says and release Quinn to do so. "Well, well, well. Look at that. My boy is a Sinner."

I shrug as I spin back to him, feeling half of the diner's customers' eyes on me. There aren't many people in this town who don't know what our cuts mean or just how dangerous we are.

"And who is this pretty little lady?" Jerry asks, dragging my attention from his customers and back to Quinn.

"I'm Quinn Renshaw," she slurs. "N-nice to meet you, J-J—"

"Jerry," he adds, helping her out.

"She needs some of your dirty fries, J."

"You got it. You want the best seat in the house."

"Do I ever not?" I wink at him.

I've been coming here for as long as I can remember. Jerry is like an adopted father to me. Hell, he treated me better than my actual old man ever did.

"Right this way then, lovebirds."

I still at his words, but Quinn doesn't. She either didn't hear him or is too desperate for food to care. She lurches forward ready to take off after him, only, her top half moves faster than her legs and she damn near faceplants the floor.

"You need me to throw you over my shoulder again, sunshine?" I ask, wrapping my arm around her and holding her against me.

I'm more than down for the suggestion. I'll be the first to admit that her ass looked fine over my shoulder. Felt even fucking better under my hand.

"I'm fine. Thank you," she states, trying to sound in control of herself.

"Fair enough."

With my hand clamped on her hip, we follow Jerry and I lead her out the back of the building to a place where most customers don't get to experience.

"Wow," she breathes as we walk out onto the deck toward a swing seat perfect for two and a small coffee table. "It's beautiful."

Looking down at her as she stares out at the vast lake before us, the water reflecting the moon above as the trees hide its magic from the rest of the world.

"Yeah," I muse, thinking that the view has nothing on her.

"You want the usual?" Jerry asks from behind us. I'd almost forgotten he was there.

"Yeah. Sodas though, no more alcohol."

"You got it, boy. Enjoy." He winks and slips back into the building.

"So what kind of favors do you have to pull to get treatment like this?"

I laugh as I lower myself to the seat, pulling her with me. "I've been coming here for years. Known Jerry since I was a kid. I guess you could say this is my happy place."

Her eyes widen at my admission.

"What?"

"Killian Crankton has a happy place that doesn't involve bikes, guns, and pussy."

I can't help but laugh at the serious look on her face as she speaks.

"You really don't think very highly of me at all, do you, sunshine?"

"Enlighten me."

"I thought I was in my happy place."

"Don't tell me that you secretly volunteer with unwanted puppies at an animal shelter and help at a soup kitchen too."

"Would it give me a better chance if I said I did?"

"No," she states firmly, but it's a lie and we both know it. And that only becomes even more obvious when she shifts over a little and leans into my side.

"Getting comfy, sunshine?"

"I'm cold, don't read too much into it."

Glancing down at the little black dress she's wearing, I realize my mistake. She's probably freezing.

Thankfully, I'm not the only one who's noticed because not a second later does Jerry appear with a tray of drinks and a blanket.

"Thanks, man."

"Fries will be a few more minutes," he says as I cover both of our legs with the heavy fabric.

"No rush. I'm sure we can find a way to keep ourselves busy."

"How many times?" Jerry says, rolling his eyes. "No sex on my swing."

A chuckle rumbles in my chest but Quinn doesn't find it half as amusing seeing as her entire body goes rigid as Jerry walks away with a smirk.

She turns to me, her cheeks red with anger, her chest heaving making my eyes drop straight to her low-cut dress.

Unlike all the other times I've seen her, tonight she looks like she'd fit right in at the clubhouse. She's got the tiny, tight dress and heavy makeup thing down to a tee.

She looks hot.

Really fucking hot.

"You bring girls here to fuck them?" she seethes.

"No, sunshine. Jerry is just yanking my chain."

"He seems to know a lot about it."

"Come here," I say, wrapping my arm around her shoulder, pulling her back into my body. "I've never fucked anyone here. Hell, I've never even brought a girl here before."

"Doesn't sound like it," she mutters under her breath.

"Are you calling me a liar, sunshine?"

"I don't know. Maybe. I don't even know you."

"Ask me anything you want, get to know me."

Ripping her eyes away from mine, she stares out over the lake as she thinks. "Why are you doing this?"

"Doing what? Waiting for Jerry's dirty fries?" I ask, knowing full well that that's not what she means.

"No. Why are you stalking me? Turning up wherever I am and..."

"And?" I urge, suddenly desperate to know what she really thinks I'm doing with her.

"Pretending to want me. Trying to drive me crazy."

"Pretending? Is that what you really think?"

"I'm in high school. I'm eighteen. I'm Micky's daughter. I'm—" Her words die when I reach out and take her chin between my fingers turning her so she has no choice but to look at me.

My eyes hold hers before they briefly flick down to her lips when she drags the bottom one into her mouth. "You think I don't know all that?" I breathe. "Trust me, I know. I've gone over it all, again and again but still, I always end up right here."

I lean forward, the temptation of having her this close to me is too much to take.

"Dirty fries for two," Jerry announces, happily ruining our moment.

"Fuck," I hiss, releasing Quinn and allowing her to shift away from me.

Jerry's knowing smirk grates on my last nerve as he lowers two plates to the coffee table before us. "Have fun kids," he says, backing away with a wink.

"We were trying." Fucking cockblocker.

"Oh my God," Quinn moans, dragging my attention to her as she licks some melted cheese off her finger.

My eyes fixate on her lips as my cock swells at the sight. "G-good, right?"

"So good."

When she drops her hand for another, I realize that she's already got her plate on her lap, but I make no move to get mine, too distracted by watching her eat.

"Don't just sit there staring," she snaps, dropping another fry into her mouth.

"Cocktease," I mutter, slipping my hand beneath the blanket to rearrange myself.

"Problem?" she asks innocently, as the fabric falls from my knees exposing my issue.

Her eyes lock on the more than obvious bulge in my pants and she swallows hard.

"Careful, sunshine, or I might start thinking you're interested."

"I'm not," she barks back quickly, too quickly.

Leaning over, I brush my lips against her ear. "So if I were to slide my hand beneath that sinful little dress, I wouldn't find you wet and ready for me then?"

Her gasp of shock pierces the air around us but she doesn't deny anything. "Crank, you can't—"

"I can, sunshine. I can do whatever the hell I want, and you know for a fact that I will. My patience for this little game you're playing will only last so long."

"I-I'm not playing a game," she argues.

"No?" I ask, pulling back from her so I can look at the top half of her dress that's not covered by the blanket. "So you didn't dress like that thinking you'd see me tonight?" Reaching out, I run my finger over the thin strap over her shoulder.

A violent shudder rips through her body, goose bumps erupting from my touch. "Y-you didn't even enter my head when I got ready to go out with my friends tonight."

"You were partying in my town, sunshine. You really expect me to believe that?"

My finger continues down heading for the swell of her breast as her breathing continues to increase.

"Believe what you want. You're not a factor in my life in any way."

Dropping my hand from her body, I snatch a fry from her plate and sit back as I throw it into my mouth. "Sure. That's why your nipples are trying to fight their way out of your dress right now."

She gasps, her hands immediately lifting to cover herself. It's not necessary, I can't actually see them, but I'm confident that I'm right.

"Eat up, sunshine. If what you're saying is true, you'll just want me to take you home soon, right?"

"You should have taken me straight home," she mutters as I finally reach for my own plate.

"Here," I pass her a fork knowing that I'm not going to be able to cope with watching her suck cheese and sauce from her fingers much longer.

We sit and eat in silence as the tension continues to crackle around us. The heat of her body burns down my side ensuring that the only thing I'm able to focus on as I slowly eat is our proximity. Of how easy it would be to lean over and take what we both clearly want.

"Is that a house through those trees?" Quinn

asks, pointing to the opposite side of the lake, clearly paying more attention to her surroundings than I am.

"Yeah. There are only three properties on this lake. One of them is derelict."

"Wow. I'd love to live somewhere this peaceful. It must be so relaxing waking up to this," she muses.

"Quieter than life on the compound that's for sure."

"You say that like you don't like it."

"Sometimes it's nice to get away from all the bikers."

"And the club whores?"

I shake my head. "You know, I'm not *that* bad."

"Sure, you are. I've lived this life since I was in diapers. I've seen more than any young girl should. I *know* exactly what you're like. Oh, I have another question," she pipes up, placing her empty plate on the table.

"Shoot," I say, although I already know that I'm going to regret it.

"How many notches on your bedpost, VP?" Her lip curls in disgust as she says my title, her eyes dropping to the patch on my cut.

"I don't know," I say honestly. "But I can tell you this," I whisper, abandoning my half-eaten fries in favor of turning toward her.

"There isn't a single one I want to remember."

7

QUINN

He's going to kiss me.

This big burly inked biker is going to kiss me.

And I'm not sure I'm going to stop him.

Crank has surprised me tonight. More than that, he's pulled the rug from right under me on my preconceptions about the kind of man he is.

I'm not foolish enough to think that the notches on his bedpost is a very healthy number, but maybe there is more to Killian Crankton than meets the eye.

He slides his hand into my hair and gently collars my throat. I didn't ever think I'd enjoy being manhandled in such an overt display of ownership, but I can't deny that my skin is vibrating with anticipation.

"So fuckin' beautiful," he leans in, whispering the words against my cheek. "I can't wait to fuck you out of my system, sunshine. To see what you look like bent over my bike, to feel your tight pussy wrapped around my cock."

What?

I blink at him, shame burning my cheeks.

He thinks I'm... like them? His club whores. Just another notch on his bedpost.

I can't believe I was actually falling for his white knight in a leather-cut routine.

"I think you should take me home." I manage to get the words out surprisingly calmly.

"But we're just getting to know each other," he drawls, running his thumb along my jaw.

"Get your hands off me" I swat him away and put some distance between us.

He sits back, running a hand down his face. "I feel like I'm missing something here. I thought—"

"You thought I was going to let you fuck me because you let me ride on the back of your bike and brought me some fries?"

"What the fuck are you talking about?" he growls, anger flaring in his eyes.

"I think your words were, 'fuck you out of my system.' Newsflash asshole, I'm not looking to be anybody's next conquest. You really should have stuck with Lucy. At least she was a sure thing."

"Are you done?"

Oh, he's pissed, alright. His nostrils flare as he glares at me.

"Yeah, I'm done."

So done.

Crank is no different to every other guy who thinks women are simply there for their entertainment and pleasure.

Screw that.

I have too much self-respect to become anyone's fuck toy.

But I can't deny the sting of disappointment at finding out he really is just like the rest of them.

"How is everything?" Jerry appears but his smile falls when he senses the tension crackling between us.

"Everything was great, thanks." I force a smile.

"Yeah, great." Crank narrows his eyes on me, but I refuse to look at him. "We've gotta make tracks, man. But I'll come around soon." He digs out his wallet and throws a twenty down on the table. "Quinn..."

Quinn, not sunshine.

Whatever. I guess it's a good thing he's putting some distance between us. We can go back to our lives—back to pretending the other doesn't exist.

It was easier that way anyway.

Jerry says good night and we make our way out of the diner. Crank moves ahead of me, practically ripping the helmet off the handlebars and thrusting it at me.

Obviously he regrets putting in so much effort with me only to find out I'm not that kind of girl. But I don't for one second think he won't find his kicks elsewhere once he takes me home.

We get situated on his bike, but Crank doesn't pull me close this time. In fact, it's almost like he's trying to get away from me. I have no choice but to clutch onto his cut, hoping to God that I manage to stay on the death machine for the entire ride.

The engine roars to life beneath us and he doesn't even check I'm okay before pulling onto the dirt track leading back to the main road.

But even over the rumble of the bike, I'm sure I hear him mutter, "Fuckin' women."

By the time my house comes into view, I want nothing more than to put this night behind me.

Riding to the lake with Crank had been exhilarating but riding home was utterly painful, each minute more excruciating than the last.

When the bike comes to a stop, I all but leap off the back. "Thanks," I mumble, thrusting out the helmet for him to take.

"What? No goodnight kiss?"

"Asshole," I seethe, and he chuckles. He freaking chuckles.

"Have a nice life, Killian." I wave him off as I head toward my house. I'm almost at the front door when I sense him behind me. Whirling around, I glower at him. "What the hell do you think you're doing?"

"What does it look like?" He moves ahead of me and knocks on the door.

I grab his arm and yank it back. "What the hell, Crank? It's late, my parents will—"

The porch light flickers to life and dread curls in my stomach. "Okay, asshole, you can go now." I spit.

"Cute, but I think I need to have me a little word with your old man."

"What?" I gawk at him like he's grown a second head. "You cannot be—"

"Quinn, is that you?" My father's gruff voice makes me go rigid.

"It's me, Daddy."

The door swings open and he frowns. "What in God's name are you—Crank?" He glances between us.

"Hey, Micky."

"Does somebody want to explain what the fuck my daughter is doing—"

"Go ahead, Quinn, explain." Crank taunts me and red-hot anger explodes in my veins.

"Well?" My dad grunts.

"Found her ass over elbow drunk at some party over in the Ridge. She was being harassed by some little punk so I figured I would do the right thing and bring her home."

I cut him with a deadly look, and he chuckles again, that deep smooth sound that does funny unwanted things to my stomach.

"She's pretty embarrassed by the whole thing, but like I told her, I'd rather make sure she got home safely than end up another statistic, you know?"

Oh. My. God.

He did not just say that.

"Is this true, Quinn?"

"No, Daddy, I—"

"Get inside. And don't wake your mom."

"If you just let me explain—"

"Inside, young lady. Now."

He wheels backward to let me past, and I stomp inside.

"Aren't you forgetting something?"

"What?" I frown back at my dad.

"You should thank Crank, he didn't need to do that."

My eyes lift slowly to Killian's, and I want nothing more than to wipe the smug smirk of his face preferably with sandpaper.

"Thank you, Crank." I give him my best saccharine smile and hurry inside, going straight up to my room and slamming the door behind me.

Leaving the light off, I slip over to the open window and listen to the men down below.

"I'm sorry you had to find her like that."

"I'm just glad I was there to step in."

Yeah, I bet you were.

"My Quinn is a good girl but she's finding things... tough since everything went down."

"I know she and Kat have hit it off, so I'll keep an eye on her."

"I'd appreciate that, Crank."

"No problem."

"Well, I guess I'd better go and deal with her teenager tantrum."

Teenager tantrum?

It sounds like I'm thirteen-year-old acting out. Not an eighteen-year-old out doing normal eighteen-year-old things.

Refusing to watch Crank ride off, I strip out of my clothes, pull on my nightshirt, and flop down on my bed.

I hear my dad struggling to climb the stairs and my heart cracks. He used to be so strong and formidable. Now it takes him ten minutes to drag himself up the stairs. I hear him panting in pain as he shuffles down the hall toward my door.

"Quinn?" He knocks quietly. "Sweetheart?"

I press my lips together, hugging a pillow to my chest as silent tears streak down my cheeks.

I don't want to talk. I don't want to hear his disappointment or see it in his eyes. So I lie there, pretending to be asleep, hoping he'll go away.

And after another whispered, "Quinn," he does.

The next morning, Dad is already gone. One of the guys from the club came by to pick him up. I heard Pacman joking about pimpin' Dad's wheelchair.

"Morning, sweetheart," Mom says as I pad into the kitchen and plop down on a stool. "Coffee?"

"Sure."

"Are we going to talk about the fact you were drunk at a club last night and Crank had to give you a ride home on the back of his bike?" She pins me with a concerned look.

"Are you giving me a choice?"

"This isn't you, baby. What's going on in that head of yours?"

"Really, Mom? You really want to go there?"

She slides a mug of coffee my way and lets out a soft sigh. "Quinn..."

"It's fine, Mom. I'm fine."

But nothing is fine.

My dad almost died, and now he has to live with life-altering injuries. My mom is barely holding it together. My best friend in the entire world is too busy playing house with her boyfriends to pick up the phone and call me. And I'm just supposed to get on with it like everything is okay.

It's all bullshit.

"Baby, look at me." Mom reaches across the counter and takes my hand in hers. Slowly, I meet her gaze. "It's been a rough few weeks, but we'll get through this, I promise. You and Dad and I are just finding a new normal."

"You're sure?" My voice cracks, and she rushes around to my side, pulling me into her arms.

"I promise. We love each other and we will get through this. All of us. But sneaking off to a bar in Red Ridge and getting drunk isn't the answer."

"Mom, I'm eighteen."

"And I remember the kinds of mistakes I made at eighteen, baby. It's senior year, I don't want you to lose focus. If Crank hadn't been there last night to bring you home—"

"Please, don't."

If only they knew the truth, I'm sure they wouldn't be singing his praises. But I'm not about to tell them. I like my freedom, and something tells me if they knew Crank and I had shared a... moment, I won't be allowed out again any time soon.

Mom brushes the hair from my face. "You're such a good girl, Quinn. I don't want you to forget who you are, okay?"

But that's the thing...

I'm not sure who I am anymore.

8

CRANK

I had every intention of riding back to the compound after being dragged out tonight. But when I left Quinn's house, I found myself heading back to this side of the Ridge.

Blowing out a stream of smoke, I sit back in my chair on my deck and look out at the world beyond. I've never fucked up that badly with a woman I've wanted before. Hell, I've never been rejected quite like that either.

I'd be lying if I said it didn't sting.

Most women melt at those dirty words and the images they conjure up in their heads. But that's just the thing. Quinn is not most women.

And she's right, she's certainly no club whore who wants to do anything for me.

She's strong. Independent. Sexy as hell.

Reaching down, I pull at my pants, needing to give my quickly growing cock some space. I thought

I was going to finally get inside her tonight. And fuck, my balls are now blue as fuck as the memory of staring right into her eyes seconds before I thought I was going to kiss her plays out in my mind.

Why did I even hesitate? I should have just done it. Taken what should be mine and claimed her as such.

But I fucking stopped to appreciate the moment like a sad fucking cunt.

I shake my head at myself wondering when I turned into such a pussy. When have I ever stopped to appreciate the moment? I just go all-in guns blazing, get what I want and get out again. That's my MO. That's what I've always done.

"How many notches on your bedpost, VP?" Her words from earlier come back to me and I scrub my hand down my face.

"Too many, sunshine," I mutter to myself, lifting my beer to my lips and taking a long pull. "Too fuckin' many."

But the issue isn't them, not really. They all said yes, and I was just along for the ride.

The problem right now is that *she* said no. The only one I ever really wanted to fall under my spell was barely affected by me and ran before the first kiss.

No one's ever said no. And I have no fucking clue how to handle it, because all it's done is make me want her more.

Pinching my blunt between my thumb and forefinger, I bring it to my lips, taking another hit, anything to help chill me the fuck out and to stop me from riding straight back to her house and taking exactly what I need. What I know we both need.

She wanted me. That I'm sure of. The way she leaned into my body, the way her eyes darkened when she looked at, how they kept flicking down to my lips.

Only, she didn't want me enough because now she's home alone in her own bed instead of mine.

Knowing the beer isn't going to be enough, I push up from the chair and go in search of something stronger.

Quinn avoided the compound all weekend despite the fact Micky was there along with Ray helping us get everything back to working order after Darren ripped through us like a fucking whirlwind.

Nolan used to have this place running like a well-oiled machine. The shop was successful and the compound itself was always in good order, but as he began to lose the fight with his health, the club seemed to crumble right along with it.

Ritz, our VP, did what he could, but with his mind constantly on his father, he was only giving the club half of himself. That allowed others—

namely Darren—to come in and begin shredding the club to pieces.

None of us even saw it happening until it was too late. And by then we were burying brothers and having to rebuild from the ground up as the Red Ridge Sinners, not the Reapers that we've always been.

Last night, we all headed into Savage Falls for Church with Ray to discuss progress and schedules for when we're going to be able to start running shipments again. We've had both Savage Falls and Red Ridge PD buzzing around us like flies since everything went down, and both businesses are suffering. We've got clients who need their supplies, and without them and their money, both clubs are going to be in trouble.

Some of the other members' kids were hanging out in the clubhouse, even Kat was there with River but still there was no sight of Quinn and it was driving me to the brink of insanity.

My need to just see her was starting to make me question my sanity.

And that's exactly why I find myself sitting in Savage Falls High parking lot on Monday afternoon like a fucking creep.

If I wasn't already painfully aware that she was too young and innocent for me, then sitting outside a high school really should have nailed the point home.

It did. Only not enough to make me kickstart

my engine and disappear in the opposite direction. Instead, I stay there, hiding in the shadows and waiting for the sight I've been craving since I left her at home on Friday night.

Knocking and alerting Micky to her antics was a dick move. I knew it when I was doing it, but I needed a reminder that she still lived at home, that she was a kid. That her dad would blow my fucking brains out if I ever did actually touch her.

Kids come and go, most climbing into their cars and disappearing for the night. I sit there for a bit reliving my high school experience. It doesn't take long, I didn't go a lot.

Finally, after almost all the other kids have disappeared, I see a familiar head full of red hair emerge from the main entrance. My heart jumps into my throat, but that excitement laced with relief at seeing her is soon replaced with anger because she's not alone.

She's with a guy. A guy who keeps looking down at her like she's the only fucking girl in the world. My fingers grip my handlebars as if it's the motherfucker's throat. He's a weed, probably on the track team or some shit, it wouldn't take long to squeeze the life out of him.

They bypass Quinn's car and head straight for another as my heart rate increases to the point I feel it in my temple.

She can't seriously be interested in this punk.

He drives a Prius for fuck's sake.

After being the perfect gentleman and opening the door for her, she drops into the passenger seat before he jogs around the hood to join her.

I should leave, I know I should. She's with a guy her own age, exactly as she should be. But instead of kicking my starter and peeling out of the lot, I hesitate and allow him to go first, praying that the overhanging tree I'm hiding under is enough to conceal me as they pass.

I give them a few seconds before following them. I keep my distance knowing that Quinn will recognize the rumble of an engine a mile off and catch me.

Trailing them all the way to the other side of town, I park down the street when Track Boy pulls onto the side of the road out the front of an arcade.

Pussy choice of a date. Be a man, dickhead.

With his hand on the small of her back, he leads her toward the entrance as I climb off my bike and head toward them. The only good thing about his choice is that there are plenty of hiding places for me to linger as I watch them laugh and enjoy themselves at the different games.

He helps her out, correcting her shooting stance—which is totally unnecessary because I know for a fact Micky taught her to use a gun years ago—putting his skinny fingers all over her, and he high fives her, giving her a wide, genuine smile when she hits the target.

All of it makes my chest ache in a way I don't like.

I move around the huge room watching them enjoying themselves and trying to convince myself to leave her to it. He's clearly no threat to her, just one to me and what I want.

Deciding it's time to stop being a totally creepy stalker, I slip out from behind the basketball throw stall I'm hiding behind and make a beeline for the exit.

My heart is in my throat by the time I get back to my bike, and I realize fast that I made the right move getting out when I did, because not even thirty seconds later, the pair of them stroll out of the arcade, completely oblivious to my stalking and head for the diner across the street.

Shaking my head, I force myself to put my helmet on, and take off. I shouldn't be here, and I certainly shouldn't be following them.

On autopilot, I cross over the Red Ridge border and open the throttle, needing some speed to force the tension out of my shoulders.

When I come to a stop, I'm hardly surprised by my location. I haven't been here for a few weeks, but it's always where I end up when things are up in the air.

Abandoning my bike, I march past the car in the driveway and let myself into the house. "It's only me," I call, knowing she'll be curious.

Walking down the hall, I come to a stop in the kitchen doorway.

"Killian," my aunt—Diesel and Kat's mom—breathes. "What's wrong?"

I look into her kind eyes and force a smile on my face. "N-nothing."

Her eyes narrow in suspicion. She knows I never come here unless something's not right.

"Do you mind, I'm just gonna..." I point out to the backyard and she nods, a concerned smile playing on her lips.

I head out to the backyard and walk over her perfectly cut lawn to the trees at the bottom just before the stream. The old swing from when I was a kid is somehow still hanging strong from the old oak tree.

I grab the rope, and tentatively lower myself to the old-faded seat. "What the fuck am I doing?"

Stalking a kid to the arcade. Getting jealous of the guy she's with. The guy she should be with.

I've got no idea how long I sit there rocking back and forth, listening to the birds in the trees and the soft trickle of the stream before me, but I'm not surprised when I hear footsteps.

"Hey, I brought you a beer," my aunt says softly, holding the bottle out for me. "You wanna talk about it?"

I blow out a long breath.

I can't.

I can't tell her what I'm doing, who I can't get out of my head.

"So it's a girl, huh?" she asks, leaning against the thick trunk of a tree and crossing her arms.

A girl. Yeah. A girl, not a woman. And there lies the damn problem.

"You know my advice when it comes to love, Killian. Follow your heart. Always follow your heart."

Looking up into her kind blue eyes, I can't help but smile. "Thanks."

"You want dinner?" She smiles back. "I've made pie."

9

QUINN

"Trent Ford is heading over here again," River whispers as we sit outside in the quad, eating lunch.

"Oh God," I angle my body away from him, pretending to be interested in my wilted chicken salad. "Has he seen me?"

"Yup, he's—"

"Hey, Quinn," he says.

"Oh, hey, Trent," I didn't see you there.

Liar.

"How's it going, Renshaw?" He smirks.

"It's... the same as yesterday and the day before that." I smile weakly.

River stifles a giggle, and I shoot her a hard look.

"What's the deal with you and Corey then? I heard him talking about taking you out?"

Guilt ripples through me, but really there's no

reason for it. There's nothing between Corey and me. It was clear after our first date at the beginning of the year that we were just friends. But when he invited me to the arcade the other day, I said yes. I thought it would help me get my mind off a certain biker.

It didn't.

"As friends," I assure him, although I regret it the second his eyes light up as if that gives him a chance.

"So have you reconsidered my offer yet?"

"Offer?" River asks.

"Yeah, I've been trying to persuade Quinn to go out with me but she's playing hard to get."

"That's not..." I let out a heavy sigh.

Trent Ford is gorgeous, and he isn't a total jerk like some of the guys at Savage Falls High, but he doesn't know when to quit.

"We could grab some food tonight and—"

"Tonight's not going to work for me, sorry. I have... a thing with my dad."

"Yeah, okay, of course." He drags a hand through his hair, a rakish grin tugging at the corner of his mouth. "Maybe this weekend?"

"Maybe."

His whole face lights up and I internally kick myself for giving him hope. Trent is like a bull at the gate, and I just waved a red flag.

Smart, Quinn. Real damn smart.

"Cool, okay. I'll look forward to it." He winks and takes off toward the gym.

"I didn't say yes," I murmur, knowing he can't hear me.

"He's cute." River grins.

"He's... a lot."

"Gorgeous. Popular. Smart. What's not to like?"

"I don't feel anything with him." I shrug, picking at my fries.

"Maybe that's because you haven't given him a chance... or maybe it's because a certain biker has caught your eye."

My eyes widen as I gawk at her. "Why would you say that?"

"I see things." It's River's turn to shrug. "And I saw Crank frog march you out of the bar."

"You did?"

She nods.

"Why didn't you say anything?"

"I was waiting for you to say something, but you didn't so..."

"I don't like Crank, River." My brows furrow as I avoid her curious stare.

"Okay. Forget I said anything, but you know, it would be okay if you did."

"He's arrogant and cocky and annoying. Really damn annoying," I add. "And he's almost ten years older than me."

"Age is just a number, Quinn. You know that."

79

Yeah. I'm not sure my mom and dad would see it like that though.

"Kat says he's a good guy."

"You guys talked about me and—"

"No, not like that." River chuckles, settling some of the nervous energy coursing through me. "She was telling me about her experiences of growing up around the club. So does this mean you do like him?"

"I... no. *No*! We're not talking about this anymore," I snap, uncomfortable with her ability to see through me.

"Okay, whatever you say." We dump our half-eaten salads in the trash can and make our way back to the building. "You're still coming to the Devil's Night thing, right?" River asks.

"I, uh... I don't—"

"Oh, Quinn, you have to come. I like Kat but she's... a lot braver than me."

"You seemed to be doing okay at the bar on Friday."

"Well, yeah, I mean, it was fun." River tucks a lock of her blonde hair behind one ear. "But it doesn't come naturally to me, not the way it does for Kat. Please come."

There's no refusing her puppy dog eyes. "Fine," I mumble. "I'll come."

"Yay." She claps. "It'll be fun. Kat says they turn the whole place into a scare house and everyone dresses up."

"I don't understand why they don't just do it on Halloween night?"

"Diesel says it because you can get up to more mischief on Devil's Night."

"Diesel said, huh?" I smirk.

"What's that look for?"

"Nothing, nothing at all." My lips pursed as I suppress a grin.

"Diesel is Kat's brother, Quinn. He isn't..." River averts her eyes.

"He isn't what?"

When she lifts them again, her expression has dropped. "He doesn't see me like that. I'm his kid sister's friend."

There's a tightness in her voice which makes me ask, "He said that?"

"Something like that. He's just so nice and kind, ya know. He reminds me of..."

"Jax?"

"Yeah." Her lips thin. "But I guess I was wrong about him, so what do I know about guys."

Jax is a prospect for the Sinners and we all thought he had a thing for River. But he blew it and broke her heart in the process.

"It's club life, Riv. All the guys are the same. Interested in the three F's. Living free. Riding fast. And fucking hard." I scowl.

"Rhett and Dane aren't like that."

"You're kidding, right?" I snort. "Those two

were some of the worst until Sadie Ray got her hooks into them."

"So what you're saying is, I wasn't the right girl to tame Jax?" Dejection washes over her.

"Crap, no, that's not... Look River, Jax is young and impressionable. The guys expect him to prove his loyalty and live like one of them."

"But he... he slept with her, Quinn. He fucked that whore like what we shared meant nothing." She inhales a sharp breath. "Like I meant nothing to him."

"I'm sorry, babe. I am." I lace my arm through hers. "Want my honest advice?" She nods and I continue, "Don't waste your time on guys from the club. They'll only disappoint you."

"Hey, Quinn." Nyla approaches me as I trade some textbooks in my locker at the end of the day. "Where's your cousin, she hasn't been in school for a few days."

I scowl, and her boyfriend, Evan adds, "Probably getting gangbanged by Noble and those Sinner assholes."

"Nice. Real nice." I roll my eyes and slam my locker shut, heading down the hall.

But when I spill outside, I realize that they're trailing after me.

"Come on, Renshaw, don't be so uptight. We're all friends."

But that's just it. We're not friends. Evan and Nyla are one of SFH's golden couples. The jock and the cheerleader. Homecoming King and Queen. Vapid, pretentious, and cruel.

Of course, part of me gets it. When people don't understand something, often their default setting is to tear it down. But love is love, and Sadie Ray is lucky enough to have found three times the love.

She doesn't care what people think, so I shouldn't.

"Hold up, Renshaw," Evan jogs up beside me. "We're not done, yet. I had a question for you." He grabs my arm and I glower up at him.

"What, Evan? I have to go."

I don't, not really. But the last thing I want is to stand around here and discuss my cousin's sex life with him and his jock jerk friends.

"Does it run in the family? I mean, we know Sadie Ray likes getting boned by three guys at once. But what about you? Do you like three dicks at once?"

"You're disgusting," I spit the words, ripping my arm out of his hold.

"And you're nothing but biker trash, Renshaw."

The rumble of a bike engine catches my attention and I glance up to find Crank's bike just beyond the school gates.

"Friend of yours?" Nyla sneers.

"Nope," I reply without missing a beat, despite the ratchet to my pulse.

Crank is here.

At my school.

What the hell is he playing at?

"Yeah right, why else would a Sinner be waiting outside? It's bad enough Sadie Ray dragged her guys here, but now we've got to put up with you—"

"Quinn?" Trent appears, casting a concerned look at me. "Is everything okay?"

"Ford," Evan grumbles.

There's no love lost between the football and basketball teams. But I've never found myself in the middle before. Not like this anyway.

For the last three years, I've managed to keep my life at high school and life at the club separate. Everyone knows I'm Micky Renshaw's daughter, but they were more interested in Sadie's escapades. She's always been the troublemaker, the rebel. Me, I prefer keeping a low profile. I have friends who aren't club kids and I make good grades and study hard. I don't flaunt the club and the kids here— most of them, at least—respect that.

"What's going on?" Before I can stop him, Trent slings his arm around my shoulder. I appreciate him coming to my rescue, but he's got to stop touching me like this. It feels too possessive and intimate.

Not to mention the fact, there's a biker behind the school gate currently glaring in our direction.

What the hell?

"I need to go," I blurt out, shucking out of Trent's hold.

Although I hurry away, I'm not quick enough to avoid hearing Evan say, "What are you doing with that biker trash, Ford? You could do so much better."

Frustration wells inside of me and tears burn the backs of my eyes. No matter what I do, what I wear, or who I'm friends with, I'll never shake the fact that I grew up in the club.

They're my family, sure. But they're not all that I am. And I want more, dammit.

I want so much more.

Which is why, as I storm out of the school gates, I don't look twice at Crank. I don't want to know why he's parked outside of my school like some kind of creeper.

He made it perfectly clear what he wants... and I'm not like that.

I'm not that girl.

Even if my traitorous body has other ideas.

———

Crank follows me all the way home. He doesn't ride at my side, instead tailing me. I don't acknowledge him, but I know he's there.

By the time my house comes into view, I wonder what he's going to do. Of course, I really want to know why he was waiting outside of school, but I won't give him the satisfaction and ask. It might give him the wrong idea. Like I care... and I don't.

You can be physically attracted to someone without liking them. In fact, I'm pretty sure hate and attraction are two sides of the same coin. I hate him but can acknowledge he's gorgeous and big and strong and—

Ugh. Stop.

I grind to a halt and whirl around, coming face to face with Crank as he sits slightly down the street, his eyes locked on mine.

Before I know it, I march toward him. "What are you doing?" I snap.

"Nice to see you too," he murmurs.

"You know, stalking can be a felony."

"Don't flatter yourself, sunshine. I was in the neighborhood and saw those little punks harassing you outside of school."

"The only person harassing me is you." I jab my finger toward him.

A slow smirk tugs at his lips and I hate it.

I hate him.

God, why did I ever let myself believe he was something more than a cocky arrogant biker asshole?

"Go away, Crank, and stop stalking me." I spin

on my heel and wave him off as I head for my house.

"And if I don't?"

That stops me dead in my tracks and I turn slowly to meet his amused expression. "Why are you doing this?"

"Because we have unfinished business, sunshine." His eyes drop down my body and lazily slide back up. Hunger simmers in his hooded gaze, and he does nothing to hide the fact he wants me.

Inhaling a shuddering breath, I lift my chin defiantly and sass, "In your dreams, asshole."

I walk away from him.

And I don't look back.

10

CRANK

By Thursday afternoon, I've just about had enough of the cat and mouse game I seem to have started.

I've spent the week stalking Quinn like some fucking psycho. I know I need to stop, but fuck. I can't help it.

Monday she was with the skinny guy at the arcade, then Tuesday after school she was with the tall guy, a basketball player maybe. Thankfully, she left alone last night, but that didn't exactly fill me with joy, especially as she saw me at the entrance and completely blanked me.

This afternoon I ended up in Church with her father and despite the fact he knew I was clock watching, he didn't finish up his business any quicker. It made me wonder if he suspected anything. I'd like to think that if he did, he'd say something. If he'd seen me loitering a little down the street from their house, that he'd have made his way out. But so far, he's not said a word, not about Quinn. He seems to have an opinion about every other thing to do with this club.

I need Dane back. We're meant to be doing this together. He wasn't meant to fuck off on an extended trip to visit Colton U with his girl and brothers.

They need to come back, and not only because I have a suspicion that Sadie might be on my side. I didn't miss the way she had my back when it came to Quinn when we all first met. She was urging Quinn to take a chance on me. Sadie might just be the push Quinn needs because hell knows I'm doing a really shitty job of it.

I throw back my fourth or fifth... Fuck it, maybe even sixth whiskey of the night when Diesel looks over my shoulder, a knowing smile pulling at his lips.

"Look out, look out, your favorite whore is about."

"Fuckin' great, just what I need," I mutter, knocking back Diesel's drink as well as my own.

"I wouldn't know what you fucking need seeing as you won't talk, bro."

"It's... n-nothing. Just VP shit."

His brow lifts as he stares at me. "Fuck off, it is. This is more than the club. Whatever this is, it's different. I've never seen you so agitated."

"Do you have to be so fucking perceptive?" I mutter.

Thanks to my shitty parent situation, it meant that Diesel and I basically grew up as brothers. I was six when I came to Red Ridge to live with my aunt and uncle. He was a baby and a good distraction for me from being dumped somewhere new with people I'd never met before.

He was a cute kid. Shame he grew up to be such a fucking smart-ass.

"I know you, bro. I know something is wrong. And it's more than just needing to get laid."

My fist curls under the table.

I really need to get fucking laid, but the woman I want doesn't seem to be willing. Just my fucking luck. The only one who's ever buried her way under the surface, has got herself into my head, is one who's not interested in even looking at me, let alone sleeping with me.

I need her.

I need to get her under me so I can get her out of my fucking head. Out of my system and get on with my life. I've got a club to run, I need to be focused, not running around thinking with my cock.

"Hey, sweetie. Long time no see," Lucy's high-pitched voice hits my ears and I just about manage to cover my scowl.

She slides right up next to me, her hand brushing over my shoulder as the other one presses against my stomach. Clearly she's forgotten how I dropped her on Friday night in favor of Quinn.

Lucy never was the smartest.

"Luce," I half greet, half groan, much to Diesel's amusement.

"Drink?" he asks, waving Tank over for some refills.

Smart boy, he knows I'm going to need a hell of a lot more to deal with this attention.

"I've missed you," she purrs in my ear, her lips brushing over my skin, I'm sure she's hoping for some kind of reaction out of me.

She gets none.

Well not for at least thirty minutes, no matter how hard she tries or how drunk I get as Tank continues to fill my glass.

It's not until the clubhouse door slams closed a little after nine o'clock when I finally thread my arm around Lucy's back and pull her closer to me. It's a dick move, but the second Quinn's eyes locked on me when she entered, I knew I had to do everything in my power to push her buttons.

She wants me. I see it in her eyes every single time she looks at me, I can read it in her body language every time we're close, yet she won't fucking admit it and it's driving me crazy.

Quinn stills just inside the clubhouse as she watches the two of us. For two seconds, she allows me to see exactly how she feels about Lucy being attached to me like a fucking leech, but then she slams down her well-constructed mask and rips her eyes away from the two of us, instead scanning the area until her gaze lands on one person.

"Hey, what's got your attention all of a sudden?" Lucy whines, shifting herself until she's sitting on my lap.

Two minutes ago, I'd have pushed her to the floor without a second thought, but now, I hesitate, waiting to see what Quinn's going to do.

The second I clock her intentions, my hand lands on Lucy's thigh and I shift her closer.

"Now this is more like it, Crank."

Even the way she says my name makes me want to rip my ears off. It makes me wonder what my drink had been spiked with the first night I decided to fuck her. I clearly wasn't of sound fucking mind.

Dropping my lips to Lucy's neck, I watch Quinn over her shoulder as she approaches Diesel and runs her hand up his arm. My entire body tenses as I watch her try to torture me. I hate that she can play me so easily but it's fucking working.

She could have tried to flirt with anyone here and I probably could have let it go, but not Diesel. I'd really hate to have to kill my brother if he decided tonight was the night to try his luck with her.

"Mmm," Lucy moans as I brush my lips against her skin. "You have no idea how badly I need you."

Her words have zero effect on me. Quinn,

however, watching her makes my blood boil and not just in a good way.

Anger slowly flows through my veins, poisoning me from the inside out. I've got no idea what she's doing here tonight, probably collecting her father who's out in the shop, despite the fact he's already organized a ride home with one of our guys.

Did she miss me today? Is she here because I wasn't waiting for her? Or am I just reading too much into it?

Lucy chats shit in my ear, but I don't hear a word of it as I track every single one of Quinn's movements. The way she throws her hair back laughing when Diesel says something even remotely funny. She bats her eyelids at him, runs her hand up his chest and smiles as if he just hung the fucking moon.

"Crank? Are you even listening to me?" Lucy whines.

"E-excuse me," I mutter, unceremoniously pushing her from my lap and not giving two shits if she lands on her feet or not as I watch Quinn saunter through the clubhouse toward the bathrooms.

I take two steps away from Lucy when she rushes to my side. "I like your thinking, Crank. You know I'm always up for it."

Needing to get rid of her, I wrack my brain for an excuse to send her away. Turning to her, I tuck my fingers under her chin and tilt her head up so she's looking into my eyes.

"I know how you like it, Luce. And do you know what I've got in mind?"

Eagerly, she shakes her head, an excited smile playing on her lips.

"Go to my room and get the lube, you know where it is."

Faster than I thought possible, she spins on her heel and damn near runs from the clubhouse. She's going to be really fucking disappointed when she gets there because I know I locked my door earlier. The thought of finding her in there, like I have in the past, naked and waiting for me, was enough to make me double-check that fucker.

The second she's gone, I turn toward the ladies bathroom and push through the door. I have no idea if any of the old ladies or whores are in there, but I've got no issue with getting rid of them if they're loitering, so I can get what I came for.

After a quick check in all the stalls aside from the one which is locked, I'm satisfied that she's the only one in here and I flick the latch on the main door to stop anyone else from joining us. Resting my ass back against the counter, I wait for her to do her thing, my heart thundering harder in my chest with every second that passes.

My heart is in my damn throat by the time the toilet flushes and her door unlocks. It's obvious the second she emerges that she's not expecting me to be in here, her eyes go wide and all the color drains from her face.

"Fucking hell, give me strength," she mutters to herself as she marches to the sink the farthest away from me to wash her hands.

"It's nice to see you too, sunshine."

"What are you doing in here?"

"Wondering why you think it's a good idea to rub yourself up against my brother when you refuse to come anywhere near me."

She stills at my words before quickly reaching to turn off the faucet and grabbing a towel to dry her hands. "None of your fucking business."

I take a step forward and her eyes flick to me before she tries looking around my shoulder to search for a way out. "Good luck with that, sunshine. You're all mine now."

"Crank," she sighs as if she's quickly running out of steam for our impending fight.

"Why did you come here tonight, Quinn? Your father is a big boy, he can look after himself."

"I know that," she snaps. "I just—"

"Missed me," I muse.

"W-what? No, not a fucking chance."

"So you weren't worried about why I wasn't waiting for you this afternoon." Her eyes narrow in frustration as I take another step toward her, forcing her to take one back. "Or were you too busy with another friend?"

Her lips part as a gasp escapes her.

"Ah, Quinn Renshaw. She pretends to be all high and mighty, acts like the big bad bikers are beneath her. But we both know the truth, don't we, sunshine."

Her lips purse in anger, her cheeks and neck turning red. "I have no idea what you're talking about," she seethes.

"No? Well, allow me to remind you about the fact it's only Thursday and this week I've seen you with not one, but three different guys."

"Wha—"

Lifting my hand, I begin counting. "Monday there was the skinny guy. Tuesday was the tall guy. And tonight... tonight it was my brother. Oh, and let's not forget that Friday night when you were—"

The crack of her palm landing on my cheek echoes around the room as our eyes lock. Both wide with shock but for entirely different reasons.

My cheek burns red hot from her impressive hit. Maybe there is a biker bitch hiding deep within her after all.

Before she can get a read on my reaction, I lift my hand, collaring her throat and slamming her back against the wall. "You just made a massive fuckin' mistake, sunshine."

11

QUINN

The air crackles between us as we stare at each other. Crank's chest rises and falls with every ragged breath. He looks like he either wants to kill me or fuck me, and the thought is both exhilarating and a little terrifying.

"Move," I hiss, needing to put some space between us.

I hate him. I hate how he makes me feel, hate how my body responds to him.

He doesn't want me. He just wants to conquer me. I'm a challenge to him, nothing more. But I don't move.

I can't.

I'm paralyzed by his hungry gaze, like I'm the meal he's ready to feast on.

"Not until you say it." A slow sexy smirk tugs at the corner of his mouth. And I hate that too.

I hate the way he melts my insides. I've never

been that girl, the one to go gaga over a guy's smile. Yet with Crank, he smiles and I forget how much I hate him, how much I hate everything he represents.

He leans in, pressing his body against mine, his hard lines fitting with my soft curves. A whimper crawls up my throat, but I trap it between my lips.

"I know you feel it, sunshine. I know if I touch your pussy right now, I'll find you hot and slick and wet."

"God, you're disgusting," I sneer, slamming a hand to his chest. But the minute I touch him and feel his shredded muscles beneath my palms, all rational thought leaves my mind.

What the hell is happening to me?

"And you're so fuckin' hot for me." He chuckles, softly pressing his mouth to my neck.

"Crank, don't—" The protest dies on the tip of my tongue as he drags his lips along my jaw and nips the skin there. Heat flashes inside of me, making my stomach clench.

"Admit it, sunshine. Admit you want me, and I'll let you walk out of here."

Pushing back into the wall, I meet his eyes. "Never."

"So stubborn," he smirks again. "I like it. But you should know, sunshine, I never back down from a challenge."

Before I can stop him, he thrusts his hand up my skirt and cups me. "Crank, what the he—"

"Fuck, baby, you're soaked." He rubs and I moan.

I fucking moan. Because although it's gross and invasive and so damn inappropriate, I have never been touched like this. So possessively, so dirty, and intimately.

And he's not even really touching me yet.

God, I'm in so much trouble.

"Your pussy wants me, sunshine. She's greedy for my fingers." He rubs harder, back and forth over my clit until my body starts grinding against him, seeking more friction.

My eyes flutter closed as I try—and lose—the last shred of my control.

I should have known. Men like Crank don't ask, they take what they want without apology.

A whimper finally escapes my lips, and he chuckles again, this time right against my mouth. "Ready to admit it, yet?"

"Fuck you," I hiss.

"Oh, sunshine, you will. One of these days, you'll be riding my dick so hard, I'll ruin you for all other guys."

"Pig," I spit and his brow lifts.

Crank slips his fingers inside my panties, pressing two inside me. My mouth falls open as pleasure tears through me.

"Yeah, you really really hate me, don't you?"

"Asshole," I murmur, my head falling back

against the wall as he works his thumb over my clit in perfect synchrony with his fingers.

It feels too good.

"Oh God," I moan, hating how needy I sound. How desperate. But I can't stop the intense waves building inside me. He's too good at this. Too fucking skilled.

"Say it, sunshine. Admit you want me, and I'll make you come so hard you see stars."

My eyes snap to his and I glower. "We don't need to talk," I sass. All I need are his magical fingers.

"But talking to you is so much fun," he teases, pressing his fingers deeper, making my legs tremble.

"More," I beg.

"Say it..."

"Crank..."

"Say. It." Anger rolls off him as he watches me come apart. I'm so close... so, so close—

Crank rips his fingers away from me and the temperature instantly cools around us.

"W-what the hell are you doing?" I was so close and now I feel nothing but the dull ache of frustration.

"You want it, baby, beg."

My eyes narrow, anger exploding up my spine. "You're a real asshole, you know that Killian Crankton."

He leans in again, pressing his hand flat to the

wall beside my head. "Doesn't change the fact you want me though, does it, sunshine?" Crank runs his nose along my cheek and kisses the corner of my mouth before pulling away. He drags his hand through his messy hair.

"You know where to find me." He winks before slipping out of the bathroom, leaving me slumped against the wall...

Wondering what the hell just happened.

"There you are," Kat says as I join her and River. "What took you so long? Diesel said you disappeared about fifteen minutes ago."

"I... I needed a girl's minute."

She nods, sipping her soda. River catches my eye and smirks. I shoot her a 'stay out of it' look but she only grins harder.

"So, the party this weekend," Kat says. "Do you have your costume yet?"

"We're really doing that?"

"Duh. It's a costume party. I have a zombie cheerleader costume you can borrow or a catwoman dress but it's latex so it's super tight."

"Of course you do." I roll my eyes. "Did you decide what you're wearing?" I ask River, and she nods.

"You could be Jessica Rabbit," Kat suggests. "I think I have a short red dress you could wear."

An idea comes to mind and I smile to myself. "Actually, I think I know what I'll go as."

"Go on then, put us out of our misery."

"Ginny Weasley."

"Isn't that the girl from Harry Potter?" River frowns.

"Yeah. I can sex it up a little." It's perfect. I don't even know if Lucy will be there but Crank will, and after the bullshit he just pulled, I intend on driving him wild.

"I think it's perfect." Kat shoots me a knowing smile. "So we'll all get ready at my house," she adds, "and then head down to the cabin together? I heard Diesel and the guys discussing this year's scare house and it sounds amazing. Then afterwards, there's a big bonfire and cookout."

"I'm surprised Diesel lets you go."

"The first year I went, he drove me straight home. But I was only twelve. The last couple of years, he's kinda accepted I'll find a way to go whether he likes it or not. Besides, I'm not a kid anymore." Kat shrugs, something catching her eye over my shoulder. "Ugh, she's such a skank. If she rubs on him anymore, she might as well fuck him right here in front of everyone."

I glance back, my stomach dropping at the sight of Lucy all over Crank again. His eyes lift and collide with mine, and I'm once again sucked into his orbit. Sliding his arm around her waist, he pulls her slender body further into his, dropping his mouth to her neck.

Asshole.

I immediately look away, jealousy coursing through my veins. His game won't work. I won't bend to his demands just because he's all over another woman. In fact, it only makes me more determined to resist him.

Not that I did a very good job of resisting him earlier.

Maybe I should take Trent up on his offer. Or hook up with Jake again.

Ugh. Who am I kidding? Neither of them light me up the way he does.

Of course the first guy to ever really make my heart pound has to be the opposite of everything I want. Everything I've always dreamed of escaping.

"Quinn?"

"Sorry, what?" I blink over at Kat, and her brows furrow.

"I asked if you want to go up to the roof and hangout?"

Peeking back over at Crank and Lucy, I watch as she takes his hand and leads him away from their friends and down the hall toward the guys' rooms.

"Quinn?"

"Y-yeah." I force down the sting of rejection and nod. "Sounds perfect."

The further away I can get from Killian Crankton, the better.

Friday at school drags. I can't help but replay what happened with Crank last night over and over in my head.

I'm a game to him.

That's all it is.

He proved that when he left with Lucy, probably to go to his room. Probably to fuck her.

Why do I even care?

If he's with her, he won't be harassing me. Yet, I can't forget how good his fingers felt touching me. How much I liked the weight of his body pushed up against mine.

I'm clearly unhinged if someone as brash and arrogant as Crank turns me on.

But whatever this game between us is, I draw the line at him with being other girls—especially Lucy.

I make my way out of school to meet up with River. Kat is picking us up. We're making an afternoon of it. Heading into Red Ridge for dinner, then we're going to Kat's house to get ready for the party.

When I reach the parking lot, my gaze goes instinctively to the gates, but there's no sign of Crank or his bike.

Not that I really expected there to be.

He finger-fucked me in the bathroom last night,

left me high and dry, and then slept with that whorebag.

I spot Kat's car and head over to them.

"Hey," they say as I climb inside. "What's up?"

"Nothing, nothing's up." I force a smile. "Actually, I was just thinking about the party later."

"You were?" Kat grins at me through the rearview mirror. She's so excited about the whole thing, it's kind of cute.

"Yup. I was wondering, is it like a club thing only or are we allowed to invite people?"

"You want to invite someone?" River asks, confusion glittering in her eyes.

"I was thinking of asking Trent."

"Who's Trent?" Kat asks.

"Just a guy that goes to our school."

"Are you sure that's a good idea?"

I'm not, but River doesn't need to know that.

Kat glances between the two of us. "Why do I feel like I'm missing something here?"

"You're not," I say.

"Right." River huffs. "So why exactly do you want to ask Trent? I thought you were trying to avoid him?"

Damn, I forgot I told her that.

"Well, I changed my mind. Trent is hot and funny, and he likes me."

And Crank was jealous when he saw me with him.

"I think it's a bad idea," River mouths as if she can hear my thoughts.

"What is?" Kat asks, keeping her eye on the stream of kids as she backs out of the parking lot.

"Nothing." I smile again, only this time it feels more genuine. "I'm excited about tonight."

"Me too." She grins. "Who knows, maybe they'll be some cute guys there."

"Err, Kat, don't you know all the guys who will be there?" River asks.

"Well, yeah. But everyone will be in costume so it makes it all mysterious and shit. Besides, it's Devil's Night. A night of mischief and mayhem. Who knows what might happen."

I know one thing.

Killian Crankton is about to get a taste of his own medicine.

12

CRANK

Reaching over, I hang off the step ladders attaching some fake cobweb shit to the rotting beams that somehow hold the roof up of this old cabin.

"Could you look even a little bit enthusiastic about tonight?" Diesel mutters behind me where he's placing light-up skulls around the attic space.

"Um... nope. You know I hate this shit," I complain.

"You're being a miserable fuck, you know that?"

"It's not like I hate Christmas," I grumble, moving my steps to continue stringing this weird shit up.

"You don't exactly love that holiday either."

"Are you surprised?" I ask, he knows as well as I do that it was three days before Christmas when my life was ripped out from beneath me and I turned up on his doorstep alone and desperate.

If it weren't for his parents, I have no idea where I'd be now. Probably dead like my parents.

"Your past doesn't have to define your future, Crank."

"Whatever," I mutter. He's always busting my balls about my attitude and general grumpiness, but I couldn't really give a shit. My balls as so fucking blue I'm sure they're about to fall off, and I fucking hate Halloween.

Diesel thinks it's because I'm scared. I'm not. I'm not a fucking pussy when it comes to this shit. I just... it's a kids holiday and I can't help feeling like I missed out on that part of my life.

"It's going to be a great night. I heard the guys talking about inviting some girls from Colton U and—"

"Why the fuck would Colton kids come here?"

"For the bad boy bikers of course," he says with a wink.

"Right. Silly me."

"Maybe one will help you end your weird-ass dry spell. What I don't get is why you don't just screw Lucy. It's not like you haven't done it before, and—"

"Are you done? I'm fed up with you psychoanalyzing me. I'm fed up with Lucy, she's boring. Been there, got the t-shirt. Not looking for a repeat."

"Exactly why you need fresh Colton pussy."

"Sure, maybe that will do it," I say, jumping

from the top of the steps and marching from the room knowing that nothing but Quinn's pussy will fix my fucking attitude.

What I need is her, but she's not exactly playing into my hands like every other woman I've ever met.

"Bar's all set," Blaze says as he and Bones load up bottles behind our makeshift bar.

Our annual Devil's Night party has been held in this old cabin for years, every year it gets more and more elaborate with both the decorations and costumes. The guys blew all the fuses in the place last night testing out all the lights, smoke machines, and moving zombies that they've filled the place with.

I take a step back and look at it all. Both floors have been sectioned off into smaller spaces, each meticulously designed to scare the living shit out of anyone who's brave enough to enter, while a bonfire roars out the back for people to hang out around once they've had enough of the scary shit.

The place looks impressive even in the light of day and I'm sure as the sun sets, it will really come to life.

"I'm gonna..." I thumb over my shoulder, more than ready to get out and get some peace before the craziness starts.

Turning my back on the guys still putting finishing touches to the cabin, I make my way out. The only good thing about tonight's party is that I can walk home. I can slip out unnoticed and fall into my own bed.

Thoughts of doing so with Quinn and her tight little pussy fill my mind. My cock jerks in my pants as I remember just how wet she was for me yesterday despite the fact she constantly refuses to accept that she wants me.

Such bullshit, and she knows it as well as I do.

The rumble of engines cuts off my thoughts and when I look up, I find two bikes coming to a stop that I wasn't expecting to see tonight.

"Stray," I shout the second he kills his engine and pulls his helmet off. "I wasn't expecting you back, man." Walking over, I hold out my fist for him to bump.

"Surprise. I couldn't miss our first Devil's Night party, bro. How's it looking?"

"Oh yeah, you know. Creepy and shit."

"Wow," Rhett Savage says, climbing off his bike and walking over. "You sound all kinds of impressed with it."

"Meh, it's not really my thing. I'm heading home for a bit, but you should go check it out. We'll catch up later, yeah?"

"Sure. It's good to see you, man."

"You too. Glad to have you back, we've missed our prez." I wink as the color drains from his face.

I get it. All of this was a bit of a shock, and he's admitted to me that he's not sure he's ready to wear the Prez patch. But it's his birthright.

He deserves it after all the shit he's been through. And we'll figure it all out together. With Ray, Micky, Savage, and the rest of our brothers.

The time of the Reapers being a dictatorship led by Darren fucking Creed is over. We're a team. A fucking family and we figure this shit out as a unit.

As Sinners.

I spend as long as I can get away with hiding at home. Eventually the music from the cabin filters down to me along with the massive flames from the bonfire and I know that my time is coming to an end. If I don't make an appearance soon then someone will come and find me and drag me out there.

I have a quick shower before pulling a clean pair of pants on, my cut, and then stuff my zombie mask into my back pocket.

That's it. That's as much effort as they're getting out of me tonight.

Stepping out of my house, I stand on my deck and look out through the trees to where the party is already raging beyond. My fingers curl around the rail as I think about Quinn already being there, wondering what costume she might have chosen for tonight.

I've got a few ideas of what I'd like to see her dressed as that's for sure.

Sucking in a deep breath, I take off across the yard before slipping through the trees and approaching the cabin that's got lanterns lighting a path all the way to the front door.

As I stare up at the old place, I can't help but be impressed. Not bad for a bunch of bikers.

Screams come from inside the building, I've got no idea if they're fake or real, but it doesn't really matter, they sound pretty authentic either way.

A couple of my brothers stop me as I make my way to the entrance, most of them running an unimpressed eye over my costume, or lack thereof, but I really couldn't give a shit about their opinion.

Finally, I manage to make my way inside and Bones slides a bottle of beer down toward me the second I come to a stop at his bar.

"Wow, Crank. You really went all out."

Pulling my zombie mask from my pocket, I pull it over my head. "Better?" I ask, although even I can appreciate that it's pathetic compared to his elaborate Dracula face paint.

"Crank!" Diesel barks from somewhere behind me, strolling over with his arm thrown around a sexy nurse who already looks drunk off her ass. "Are you shittin' me, bro?"

"Leave me the fuck alone," I mutter, downing my beer and gesturing for another. "Who's this?" I ask, nodding toward his girl.

"C-Carly?" The fact it comes out as a question makes me smirk. She doesn't seem so amused by it.

"It's Kelsey," she hisses. "I literally just told you."

"Babe, I'm sorry," he pleads but it's too late. She's already ducked out of his hold and stormed off.

"Seriously?" he barks, hitting me upside the head and dislodging my mask.

"Because it'll be so hard to find another, Captain Jack."

He flips me off and disappears, muttering, "you're ruining my game."

"You need to get laid," Bones says, passing me two beers this time. Apparently, I look like I need them.

"What I need is for everyone to get off my fuckin' case."

His brows rise in surprise. I don't often lose my shit with the guys but it's getting harder and harder to keep my cool these days.

Spinning around, I rest my ass against the bar and scan the crowd making their way in and out of the different scare rooms. Most are laughing and joking, but there are a few, mainly females, who look scared out of their minds. Pussies.

Watching everyone enjoy themselves almost makes turning up worth it and I'm just starting to relax a little when two people I recognize appear in the doorway.

Kat and River are wearing matching vampire cheerleader costumes. I watch them, my heart racing as I wait to see if Quinn is going to emerge with them. I know they were all getting ready together, Diesel let it slip earlier that they'd taken over my aunt's house and forced him to go out to get away from the girly excitement.

Tipping my bottle to my lips, I wait as they disappear into the crowd, my eyes locked on the door. My grip on my bottle tightens the second she emerges, but it's not because of her outfit, which incidentally, is sexy as fuck. It should be the reminder I need that I should be walking away from her, but all it does is make me want her more.

The short tartan skirt sits high on her thighs, if she were to bend over then everyone in the room would get a look at what she's hiding beneath. Her white shirt is almost totally unbuttoned and tied under her breasts, showing off her slim waist. Over her shoulders is a cape, which I find a little weird for a schoolgirl outfit, the wand in her hand makes me frown too but I don't care enough to really think about it because my biggest issue about how she's just arrived is that she's on the fucking arm of that prick she was talking to after school the other day.

My knuckles turn white, my grip tight enough that I'm waiting for the bottle to shatter beneath my fingers any second as her eyes move from laughing at something the preppy prick said and immediately finding mine.

All the air rushes from my lungs as the air between us becomes charged as our contact holds.

Lifting my brow, I shoot a look at her date. "Cute," I mouth before shaking my head and pushing from the bar, pretending that I don't really care.

She's soon going to discover that it's far from the truth.

I'm in no rush, we've got all night. I'll even allow her to enjoy herself and make her date think that he's got a chance.

We both know he doesn't.

She's using him to get to me. I'd put money on it, just like I've done with Lucy.

I deserve it after I made it look like I took her down to my room to fuck her six ways from Sunday last night. But that's far from what happened in reality.

I slip into the darkness, checking out each room and laughing every time some poor unsuspecting person damn near shits their pants when a zombie or two jump out at them from the dark corners of the room.

Then I find somewhere to wait because I know that she'll end up here at some point, and when she does, she's mine, and I can guarantee that her little date will be long forgotten.

13

QUINN

"Holy shit, this place is off the hook." Trent gawks at the scene in front of us. His fake blood coated fangs peek out from under his lips as he lets out another low whistle. "This is going to be so freaking awesome."

I wish I could agree.

But on the drive over here, it became apparent that maybe this wasn't such a good idea. Trent sat a little too closely, touched me a little too much. But I guess I only have myself to blame for not correcting him when he referred to tonight as a date.

River throws me a knowing look and I glower back at her. Thankfully, she hasn't revealed the truth to Kat yet as to why I was so insistent on inviting Trent.

It seemed like a good idea at the time, when I was still majorly pissed at Crank and his little games. But now we're here, I realize I'm way out of my league.

The old, abandoned cabin is already crammed full of people, music pumping out of hidden speakers loud enough to drown out the chatter but not loud enough to disguise the screams overhead.

"Wow, what is that?" River asks, glancing toward the ceiling.

"Told you, the guys go all out." Kat grins proudly. "I'm going to get a drink, you guys want?"

"Hell yes," Trent says, taking off after her.

"Okay then." I roll my eyes and fall into step beside River, who looks super hot in her sexy zombie cheerleader costume.

"He's... eager." She laces her arm through mine.

"Ugh. Don't. He's like a kid on Christmas morning."

"Oh my God, Sadie?" River pulls me toward a dark corner of the room and sure enough there stands my cousin in all her zombie bride glory.

"You're here," I blurt out.

"Nice to see you too, cous." She pulls me into a hug. "Surprise."

"Sorry, I just wasn't expecting to see you. I thought you didn't get back until tomorrow."

"Yeah, well, we decided Dane should be here." She glances over to the bar where I spot River's brother with Dane and Wes talking to Diesel and... Crank.

Ugh.

"What's that look for—oh." Sadie smirks. "I see you're still pretending not to like him."

River snorts at that and I pin her with a disapproving look. "What?" She shrugs. "It's the truth."

"It's not. Actually, I'm on a date."

"A date?" Sadie's face crumples. "With who?"

"Trent Ford," River beats me to it.

"Trent? Wow, okay. That's... wow."

"What?" I hiss. "There's nothing wrong with Trent."

"So you didn't invite him just to piss Crank off?"

"What? No!"

Sadie's lips twist with amusement. "Sure whatever. But you know what they say, babe. Play with fire and you'll most likely end up burned. Ooh, cocktails." She barges past me to meet Wes who hands her a bright green concoction.

"Does that have eyeballs floating in it?" I ask, peering into the glass.

"Yep. It's eyeball swamp juice."

"Sounds delicious." I retch a little.

"Mmm, it's sweet." Sadie Ray shakes her head, smacking her lips together.

"Just like you." Wes grabs her jaw and kisses her hard, all teeth and tongue and far too much PDA for my liking.

"Okay then," I say, my chest tightening. "I'll be over there, getting a regular drink."

"Good luck with that," Wes says. "Everything is themed. Even the kegger has been dyed dark red." Wes holds up his glass and sure enough, it looks like fresh blood.

"I think they have Zombie Punch, that should be a safe bet." River moves ahead of me, and I use her as a shield to avoid making eye contact with Crank.

It was bad enough when I arrived and he saw me. The heat in his eyes had almost been enough to melt me on the spot. Until he saw Trent and his lust turned to red hot anger.

But a little taste of his own medicine won't hurt him.

"What the hell are you wearing?" Rhett is on River's case the second we reach the makeshift bar.

"Don't start." She waves him off. "It's a party, everyone is dressed up."

"I'm not," he grumbles.

"Yeah, because you're a boring motherfucker." Dane slings his arm around Rhett's shoulder. "Let her live a little. It's a club party, how much trouble do you think they can get into?"

"A lot. We plan on getting into a whole lot of trouble." Kat grins, flashing both Rhett and her brother a cheeky smile.

"Seriously, Diesel, man. You need to handle that, because I don't want Rive—"

"Okay, Mr. Party Pooper," Sadie appears, wrapping her arm around Rhett's arm. "It's a party, we came to enjoy ourselves. And I seem to remember you saying you'd take me through the scare house."

She leans up and kisses him, long and lingering, enough to make me and River blush. But not Kat. She wolf whistles then drains her drink, immediately asking the bartender—a rather realistic looking werewolf in a Sinners cut—for a refill.

"You need to watch her," I overhear Crank say to Diesel.

I peek up at him, I can't help it. Our eyes lock and I see his flare with lust again as he lets his gaze drop slowly down my body. But Trent chooses that exact moment to return, a goofy grin on his face as he sips his funky looking drink.

"It's witches' brew. Want some?"

Crank snorts, and I shoot him daggers.

"No, I'm good," I reply. "We should check out the rest of the house."

"Hell yeah. I was talking to Lucy and she said they even have animatronic zombies."

"L-Lucy?" my eyes widen, disbelief coating my words.

"Yeah. we got to talking at the bar."

"I see." My teeth grind together so hard I'm surprised I don't crack enamel.

"Why, do you know her?"

"Something like that." My gaze flicks to Crank, but he isn't looking at me. He's glaring at Trent, who is completely oblivious.

"Who's your friend, Renshaw?" Dane asks me.

"Oh, this is Trent. He's in our class."

"Hey, man." Trent thrusts out his hand and Dane frowns.

"Hey." He shakes Trent's hand, a faint smirk tracing his mouth. "So are you two—"

"Friends," I rush out. "We're friends."

"I'll be around," Crank announces to no one in particular. "Catch you later, Prez."

I don't think it will ever sound right hearing Dane being called that. He's barely older than me and Sadie and he's responsible for an entire chapter of the Sinners now. But he isn't alone. He has my cousin, Rhett, and Wes by his side. His family. Not the one who abandoned him, but the one who chose him. And now he has a group of guys loyal to him, willing to follow his every command.

A bloodcurdling scream rings out overhead, making me startle. Trent slips his arm around my shoulder and says, "Don't worry, I'll protect you." Everyone chuckles.

Everyone except Crank who has paused, his eyes fixated on where Trent is touching me.

Take that asshole.

I pin him with a hard look. His brow quirks a little as he brazenly holds my stare. Good thing everyone is too busy discussing what spooky delights we'll find upstairs to notice.

"Ready, babe," Trent hugs my shoulder, and I glance up at him.

"Sorry, what?"

"I asked if you're ready to go explore."

"Uh, sure."

I look back expecting to find Crank scowling at me.

But he's gone.

———

The strobe lighting is enough to give me a headache, but it does a great job of sending my heart into overdrive as we move through the room, trying to avoid the booby traps.

"AHHHHH," Trent shrieks as a zombie lurches out of a closet, smacking him on the shoulder. "Holy shit, I didn't... fuck."

"You good?" Kat asks him, hardly able to contain her laughter.

"It just caught me by surprise," he mumbles, raking a hand through his hair. "Why don't you two go ahead?"

"Yeah, whatever." Kat grabs River's hand and leads her deeper into the shadows. Fake cobwebs hang from the beams, making it hard to navigate the way.

"This is so fucking awesome." He squeezes my hand, the one he's refused to let go of since we came up here.

I force a smile, hoping he can't see the discomfort in my eyes. It's not that I'm scared, I'm not. But I know with absolute certainty my plan has backfired. Trent is like a dog with a bone, touching me, holding my hand, and acting all Neanderthal.

I didn't want to lead him on, but Crank got under my skin and I just wanted to play him at his own game.

The room grows narrow, but I realize that it's been divided using sheets of drywall. Fear races down my spine as the walls begin to close in on us, at least, that's what it feels like. Huge sheets of blood splattered plastic flap in the... wind?

My eyes squint for the source of the sudden breeze. Rationally, I know it's a blower or some kind of fan. But irrationally, my mind conjures up a hundred scenarios that all make the hairs on the back of my neck stand to attention.

Suddenly, I realize that Trent is in front of me. So much for being a gentleman. He keeps a firm grip on my hand, but something leaps out of the darkness and he screams like a little bitch, releasing me while I jerk backwards.

Strong hands grab me, pulling me into and through one of the plastic sheets and a palm comes up around my mouth, muffling my own screams.

I can't see, can't hear a single thing over the roar of blood in my ears. I can only feel him.

Crank spins me around, keeping his hand on my mouth and then leans into me, pressing me up against the wall. His dark eyes glitter under the intermittent strobe light, making him look dangerous.

He's trapping me between the wall and his big strong body. I don't even fight him this time because deep down, this is what I wanted. I wanted him to seek me out. To chase me. Even if Sadie Ray is right.

Play with fire and you get burned.

But maybe I want to go up in flames.

The air turns unbearably thick around us. Crank keeps his hand on my mouth, reaching out he trails his finger down my cheek, following the curve of my neck and down between the valley of my breasts. My breath hitches at his gentle touch.

"You look fuckin' sinful," he whispers, his voice rough as he lets his eyes fall down my body. "I needed to get a little taste."

My heart gallops in my chest, waiting for his next move. Silently praying he'll touch me again and finish what he started last night.

He drops to his knees, hikes my skirt up, and buries his face in my pussy, inhaling deeply.

"Oh God," the words fall from my lips as he licks me over the damp material, before tugging the lace again and pushing his tongue inside me.

Crank grabs my leg and pulls it over his shoulder, eating me like a man starved. But it's not enough. I need him to tear my panties off and really taste me. I'm desperate for it, my fingers buried in his hair, urging him closer.

"Quinn?" A voice pierces the air. "Quinn? What the hell, she was right here?" Trent says, and Crank goes deathly still.

Slowly, he lowers my leg and slides back up my body, pinning me with a murderous glare. "You made a mistake bringing him here, sunshine."

"I—"

"Quinn?" River calls. Kat too.

My heart is crashing so hard against my chest, I feel a little lightheaded.

What the hell am I doing?

I push him off me and stagger away, trying to search for the gap in the plastic sheet, but Crank snags my wrist.

"Get rid of the douchebag, sunshine," he demands.

"You're not the boss of me." I internally cringe at my lame comeback, but he's got me all tied up in knots.

Crank smirks and my stomach sinks. Then he says two little words that make my heart flutter.

"We'll see."

14

CRANK

The second I make my way back to the bar, I discover that she wasn't joking with her defiance because she's on the makeshift dancefloor with the dickhead she brought with her. Moving her body to the beat and allowing him to touch her as they dance with River, Quinn, Sadie and Wes.

A drink lands before me, some weird green looking shit and I immediately turn my nose up. "What happened to the beer?" I snarl.

"You drank what we had left, suck it up, VP."

"Fuck's sake," I complain, lifting the god-awful looking drink to my lips. "Wait. Is that an eyeball?"

"What did you think we did with all our enemies' eyeballs this year, Crank?" Axe deadpans.

"Suck a joker," I mutter, risking it and downing the drink.

Surprisingly, despite the color it's actually

pretty good, and strong, which is a bonus. I'm going to fucking need it by the looks of it.

Licking my lips, I discover that the taste of the drink isn't the only thing that's lingering because the sweetness of Quinn's pussy once again fills my mouth. I may have made a mistake, I think as I pull at my pants, allowing my aching cock some space.

I thought putting my mouth on her, building her up to the point of no return for the second time in twenty-four hours was a surefire way to make her leave with me.

How fucking wrong was I?

Reluctantly, I look over my shoulder. My eyes immediately land on her.

She's standing with her back to the douchebag, her ass pressed right up against his cock as she grinds her hips. My jaw clenches until it starts to hurt as I watch them, watch him with his possessive hold on her hips, ensuring that she doesn't move an inch from him.

Fucking asshole.

I slam my glass down behind me, my grip on it almost enough to shatter as she drops down low. Looking over her shoulder, her eyes find mine.

She knew I was watching.

A smug grin pulls at the corner of her lips as she slowly lifts her ass, dragging it up the prick's body.

I shake my head slowly in warning, my eyes narrowing. She's going to fucking regret this when I do finally get my hands on her. And I will. Because there is no fucking way she's leaving this place with anyone but me tonight.

I sense someone come to join me at the bar, but I'm still too distracted by Quinn to turn around.

"Yo, VP," someone barks before a sharp slap lands on the side of my head.

"What the—" Turning around, I find an amused looking Dane staring at me with a knowing glint in his eyes.

"Hey, you seem... distracted."

"Just enjoying the party, man."

He glances over my shoulder, taking in the scene that I was only moments ago. "Sure," he says, winking. "So how have things been?"

"Yeah, good. Micky has been helping reboot the shop and get things moving in the right direction. What about you, have fun in Colton?"

A look crosses his face, one I recognize all too well. "Man, you have no idea." Lifting his hand, he rubs the back of his neck as he glances toward where his girl is dancing with Wes.

"Things are good with the four of you then, I take it."

"Good? Fuck, bro. I never knew things could be this fucking incredible."

He winks, telling me he's caught her eye, and as much as I want to turn and see the look on Sadie's face, I know that I'll get stuck on Quinn long before that happens.

"I'm happy for you. She seems like one hell of a girl."

"She is. We're a good team. So what about you?"

"What about me?" I ask, trying to play it as cool as possible. Reaching for a fresh drink I take a sip.

"Well, it seems your little crush on Quinn hasn't vanished in the time I've been gone."

"W-what?" I ask, damn near choking on the eyeball.

He chuckles to himself. "All the answer I needed, man. She still holding out on you? I'm not really surprised, she's always had a stick up her ass thinking she's better than us."

My brows furrow. "S-she doesn't—"

His eyes widen, urging me to continue trying to protect her but I slam my lips shut. He's right after all, she does think she's above dating a biker. It's one of the reasons I want to prove her wrong.

"She's rebelling. She'll soon figure out that this," I say, throwing my arm out. "Is exactly where she belongs."

"You mean this world or right by your side, Crank?"

"Uh..." I down the rest of my drink, although from the shit that's coming from my mouth, I already fear I might have had one too many. What is even in this shit anyway?

"The club, Prez. She belongs here, just like your girl."

His eyes drift at the mention of her once more and this time, I can't help but turn around and watch right alongside him.

My fists curl when I find that Quinn has turned around in the dickhead's grip, he's now got his hands on her ass and is looking down at her like she's his whole fucking world.

Get a hint, prick. She's fucking not.

"Damn, you've really got it bad, huh?" Dane mutters before his eyes move to something over my shoulder.

The warm touch of hands startles me a beat before her sweet perfume hits my nose. I don't bother trying to hold back my groan of frustration as Lucy wraps her arms around my neck and presses her breasts against my back.

"Hey, I've been looking for you," she purrs in my ear.

"I haven't been hiding," I say, my voice void of any kind of excitement about her 'finding' me.

"I thought you were going to jump out of the shadows in the scare house and have your wicked way with me."

Any kind of desire that was coursing through my body courtesy of watching Quinn dance is immediately wiped out. Dane watches the two of us with amusement written all over his face. Apparently, it's only Lucy who's oblivious to how I really feel about her.

"Do you mind, Luce. Prez and I were talking about important shit."

"We were?" Dane asks, a wicked glint in his eyes that makes my jaw clench.

This asshole is meant to have my back.

"I've actually got something I need to do." His eyes return to the dancefloor before he drains his red drink and disappears into the crowd.

Great.

"Come dance with me," Lucy demands in my ear.

"I'm good, thanks."

"Come on, it's a party." She slips around me, coming to stop between my parted thighs. "I wore something special for you beneath this," she says, gesturing to her French maid costume.

My skin tingles and a ripple of awareness runs down my spine. I don't need to turn around to know that Quinn is glaring daggers at me.

Jealousy really does look good on her.

I'm expecting to have to get rid of Lucy on my own, so when someone else approaches us and says my name, my brows rise.

"Crank," Sadie says with a smile. "Do you mind if I borrow your girl here?"

"N-no, feel free."

Sadie threads her arm through Lucy's and damn near drags her to the other end of the room and around the corner.

Weird.

When I turn back, I find that Dane's vanished but he's not the only one because Quinn is now dancing with Kat and River.

Needing some fresh air, I push from the stool and start toward the exit. If it weren't for Quinn, I'd have already found my way home by now. But there's no way I'm leaving without her.

"Oh, no you don't," Diesel says, pressing his hand to my chest and forcing me to back up as I try to make my escape. "We're dancing."

"We're fuckin' not."

"Oh? But your girl is all alone and from what I can tell, her boy has downgraded."

My brows pull together, and I immediately spin around to find out what he's talking about.

"Holy shit," I breathe.

In the time it took for me to finish my drink and walk over here, Lucy has re-emerged along with Quinn's little date and well... safe to say he's not coming up for air anytime soon.

"Dane said you can thank him later," Diesel mutters, taking off toward where the girls are.

He immediately grabs his sister, spinning her around until she looks like she's about to vomit all over her cheer costume. I watch them for a few seconds, or more so, River as she stares at Diesel with a soft smile playing on her lips.

But all too soon, my eyes find Quinn again.

She's standing stock still while everyone moves around her staring at her 'date' with a deep scowl on her face. The second I take a step closer, her eyes find me. They widen and she takes a step back.

She knows exactly what this means.

Shaking her head slowly, she backs up as I continue to move toward her. "Looks like your boy's upgraded, sunshine."

Quinn pulls her arm back as if she's about to slap me but I'm faster and I grab her wrist, pulling her into my body and forcing her to move in time with the music.

"You really don't want to do that, *Ginny*."

"I'll do whatever the hell I like," she hisses, her voice slightly slurred but not enough to be unaware of everything she's doing right now. "You might not have noticed, but I don't follow your orders."

"And aren't you regretting it? If you'd done as I said earlier then you'd already be short of your preppy date and you might have already had one, maybe even two, orgasms."

"I don't want—"

Reaching up, I take her chin between my fingers. "Go on, sunshine. Keep lying to yourself." I narrow my eyes at her. "I fuckin' dare you."

Her chest heaves and her nostrils flare as she glares at me.

Leaning in, I brush my lips against her ear, loving how her body sags against mine as I do. "But don't forget, I know exactly how much you want my tongue back on your cunt. And something tells me that it's desperate for my cock too."

She tenses once more, and I get ready for her next violent reaction to my words.

"So go on, lie to me and tell me that you're not wet." Pushing my arm between us, my fingertips brush the top of her thigh before dipping under her obscenely short skirt.

"Crank," she whimpers as I connect with her damp panties.

"Yeah, exactly as I thought, sunshine."

Tucking the fabric aside, I run my finger through her folds as everyone continues to dance around us, oblivious to what we're doing.

Her hands land on my shoulders, as I push lower, dipping my finger inside her. "Y-you can't—" she tries but her words vanish the second I push inside her.

"Can't I?"

"Oh God."

"If I wanted to, I could make you come apart right here in the middle of all these people. Is that what you want, or would you rather I take you somewhere a little more private?"

Her pussy floods with heat at my words and I can't help but smile. She might claim to be different to all the others, but right now, she's nothing but a biker whore. *My* biker whore.

I finger-fuck her until she's about to fall and

just as her eyes begin to close, ready to ride it out, I rip my finger from her body.

Her eyes fly open in shock just in time to watch me push the digit past my lips and suck it clean.

Fuck.

My cock jerks in my pants, already past the point of being desperate for this woman.

This ends.

Right fucking now.

15

QUINN

Oh. My. God.

I can't believe he just did that.

I can't believe I *let* him do that.

My skin hums with anticipation, a tight knot of frustration balled deep in my stomach. I was close... so damn close to that rush of ecstasy, the moment when nothing else exists except pure bliss.

It's wrong, all kinds of wrong, since the party is going on around us, with people potentially watching. But now I've felt his touch, felt those magical fucking fingers again, the last of my resolve crumbles around me.

But I can't do this... can I?

The air crackles between us as Crank watches me.

No, watching me doesn't do justice to the way his eyes burn into mine, searing me right down to my very soul.

"We're leaving," he says in a rough, demanding voice, as he takes my hand.

"Wait." I pull back sharply, inhaling a small breath.

"Don't make me wait, sunshine," he drawls, "because I'm about ten seconds away from taking you right here in front of everyone and I'm not sure you want your friends to watch me fuckin' you."

His dirty words make my stomach clench.

How can he make something so illicit sound so good?

A beat passes. And another as my head, heart, and body go to war.

My head knows it's a mistake.

My heart knows it'll end up a casualty of Killian Crankton.

But my body—my needy, desperate body—wants this.

It wants him.

"I—"

"Yo, Crank, my man." A big hairy werewolf slings his arm around Crank's shoulder. "This party is off the chain."

"I'm kinda busy." His eyes flick to mine but I use the moment to make a dash for the door.

I don't glance back as I hurry from the party, spilling out into the inky night in a rush of adrenaline. I don't know where I'm going but I need to get away from Crank and the confusing things he makes me feel.

Staggering toward the tree line, my heart races in my chest as I try to figure out a plan.

I can't stay here. If I do, I'm going to end up giving in to him.

"What the fuck," Crank snaps as he bursts from the cabin. Our eyes lock and I see the demand there.

Don't run.

But with a shake of my head, I make a dash for it, running into the darkness of the trees. Crank groans from somewhere behind me, his heavy footsteps telling me he's giving chase.

Shit.

I can barely run, staggering through the undergrowth, clutching trees and branches as I try to put more distance between us.

"I know these woods like the back of my hand, sunshine." His dark chuckle echoes around me and I freeze, turning on the spot, trying to figure out which direction he's coming from.

Realizing I'm at a huge disadvantage, I tuck myself behind a giant tree, pressing my body flat against the rough bark. Maybe he'll walk right by me, get bored of looking and go back to the party.

My heart crashes violently against my chest as I try to swallow the whimper crawling up my throat. Everything is quiet, no sound of his boots or leaves crunching beneath them.

Maybe he's gone. Maybe he doubled back.

I inch around the tree and strain against the darkness, searching for—

"Got ya." Big hands grab me and pull me backwards against his hard chest. "You ran."

His voice sends shivers down my spine, and I steel myself as I turn slowly in his arms to meet his thunderous glare.

"I can't do this." I yank out of his hold and back up, putting space between us. But Crank follows, taking one step forward for every step back I take.

"This, you and me," he wags his finger between us, "is happening. One way or another, sunshine, I am getting inside you tonight."

"Do you have to be so—"

Crank is in front of me in a second, his big imposing frame looming over me. "You were saying?" He smirks as I gawk up at him.

"I hate you," I spit the words.

"That might be so, *Ginny*, but it doesn't change the fact your pussy wants me."

God, he's an asshole.

An infuriating, cocky asshole.

"Unless you want me to scream, you should probably leave," I sass, immediately realizing my mistake when his lips twist in amusement.

"Oh, you'll be screaming by the time I'm through with you."

"You're deluded if you think I'm going anywhere with you." I almost sound convincing as I barge past him.

But Crank's hand shoots out, grabbing my wrist.

"What the hell are you—"

"Fuck it." Crank scoops me up and throws me over his shoulder.

"Seriously, Crank," I hiss. "Put me down." My hands slam against his back but he doesn't relent, walking deeper into the dense trees. The shadows swallow us whole, but Crank navigates the route with ease.

"Okay," I sigh dramatically. "You made your point, you can point me down now."

"And risk you running off again?" He chuckles and it's so dark and wicked it makes butterflies erupt in my stomach. "Not a chance." His hand slips under my skirt and grabs my ass making my breath catch.

"You like that, baby?"

"You're such an asshole."

"But you love it." His fingers inch higher, brushing my panties, and I smother a whimper.

Why?

Why does it always feel so good when it's so wrong?

The trees grow thinner and another cabin appears.

"Welcome home," he says teasingly, but there's something in his voice that makes my heart flutter. Something I refuse to acknowledge because this is a game.

I'm the mouse and he's the cat, and once he's caught me, I don't doubt he'll lose interest.

But maybe that's for the best. Maybe we both just need to get this weird connection simmering between us out of our systems and then move on with our lives.

Crank carries me up the small steps leading to his porch and finally lowers me to my feet. Staring down at me, I feel stripped bare under his intense gaze.

"What?" I whisper, nervous energy zipping through me.

"The things I'm going to do to you." His voice is thick with need as he reaches out and traces my jaw with his finger. "Ready to be fucked by a dirty tatted biker?" He smirks.

"You're disgusting." I roll my eyes. I do that a lot around him.

"That might be so, sunshine." Crank crowds me against the wall, his arms caging me in. "But we both know that it gets you hot."

One of his hands dives under my skirt and he cups my pussy, rubbing me.

"God," I breathe, arching into his possessive touch.

"You can call me God any day of the week." He claws at my panties until two of his thick fingers impale me.

"Fuck. That's... fuck." My eyes roll again, my head falling back against the wall as he works me hard and fast, fucking me with his fingers like he hates me.

And maybe he does.

Maybe he hates this thing between us as much as I do.

Liar.

Because I don't hate it, not even a little bit.

His thumb teases my clit and I ride his hand, needing more.

"Jesus." His other hand slides to my throat, collaring me. "You are so fuckin' hot. I can't wait to slide inside you and feel your tight pussy choking my cock."

Crank kisses me. Devours me with his teeth and tongue, refusing to let me come up for air as he gently squeezes my throat. Adding another finger, he stretches me to the point of pain, but I'm so lost to the sensations coursing through me that I can barely remember my name.

"Come," he demands, pinching my clit hard. A wave of pleasure rolls through me as I tremble around him, my knees buckling from the sheer force of my orgasm.

"Holy shit," I pant, sagging against the wall. "That was—"

"Just the beginning." He releases me and digs out his wallet, unlocking his door. Grabbing my hand, Crank pulls me inside and I stumble behind him, still breathless and unsteady from his touch.

The door clicks shut behind us, piercing the air like a gunshot.

"You live here?"

It's a stupid question but I need a moment. I need to get my head on straight before—

"No distractions." He prowls toward me.

"What, you're not going to offer me a drink or something to eat?"

His brow quirks up. "The only thing I'm going to be eating... is you."

"Original," I murmur.

"But first." Crank snaps open his belt and pushes his jeans off his hips slightly, grasping his hard length. Thick and long, he fists his cock, gritting his teeth as he tugs. "On your knees."

When I don't jump to his demand, his eyes darken. "You have two choices, sunshine. Get on your knees and put those pretty lips on me or I get on my knees and feast on your pussy bringing you to the edge over and over until you're a writhing desperate mess... your choice."

"You're a bastard, you know that, right?"

"So you keep saying." He smirks, lazily jerking himself off. "But if you want me to get you off, which I will, all night long, I'm going to need you to... Get. On. Your. Fucking. Knees."

"So bossy," I sass.

I like this game. It makes things less confusing. It's just sex.

Hot mutual sex.

A sexual exorcism if you will.

I can do this.

I can exorcise him right out of my system and get an orgasm or two out of it.

Sinking to my knees, I crawl toward him, putting on a show. Confidence courses through my veins as I watch the hungry expression on his face. The second I'm close enough, Crank winds his fingers into my hair, guiding my lips onto his cock.

"Open up, baby."

Closing my fingers around his shaft, I flick my tongue over his slit, tasting him. He groans, low and throaty, and I take him deeper, revelling in the way he responds.

"Fuck yeah," he grits out, thrusting into my mouth. "That feels so fuckin' good."

I work him over with my hand and mouth, pumping him harder and faster as I hollow my cheeks and take him as deep as I can until I'm gagging around him.

"Shit..." he chokes out, hitting the back of my throat. "That feels... *fuck*."

Crank's hips buck wildly as his grip on my hair tightens and I know he's close. His legs lock up as he begins to lose control...

And right at the last second, I pull away, smiling up at him.

"What the fuck?" he growls.

"Payback's a bitch." I leap to my feet and take

off toward the stairs. If I wanted to escape, I'd run for the door.

The truth is though, I don't want to escape.

I want him to catch me.

I'm tired of fighting it, fighting him.

For one night only, I want to give in.

I want Killian Crankton to rock my world.

But first, he'll have to catch me.

16

CRANK

My chin is damn near on the floor as I watch her flee from the room and dart toward the stairs. Her evil laughter floats through the air as she disappears from my sight.

Heat courses through my veins, my cock bobbing hard and angry in front of me.

I was so close. So fucking close.

"You're going to regret that, sunshine." My deep voice booms through the house as her tiny feet pound on the floorboards above my head.

My mouth waters, my fingers curl as images of all the things I could do to her when I catch her flicker through my head.

Shrugging out of my cut, I move toward the stairs, more than ready to hunt down my prey and finally make her mine.

I take off up the stairs. "You can't hide from me,

sunshine," I warn, my voice low and deadly as the floorboards creak beneath me. Just like downstairs, none of the lights are on, making this little game all the more exciting.

"Come out, come out wherever you are." I have to fight not to laugh as I push the guest bedroom door open and see nor hear any movement inside. Not that I really thought she was there.

Anyone running always goes for the farthest room, right?

Even still, I make a show of opening each door, even the closet, just to build the tension. When I get to her, I want her desperate, dripping for us to continue where we left off.

"Sunshine," I sing, approaching the master bedroom which covers the entire rear end of the house, the balcony looking over the lake beyond.

I hear her in the silence the second I step over the threshold. Her breathing is too ragged to stay hidden.

I round the bed and march straight for the open bathroom door. "Am I close, sunshine?" I tease.

A quiet whimper fills the room.

"The things I'm going to do to you when I catch you." I take another step forward. "I'm going to start by stripping you naked. The Ginny look is hot, really fuckin' hot, but I want you, Quinn. Every fucking inch of you."

Whimper.

"I'm going to run my lips, my tongue, my fingers over your perfect skin, drive you crazy."

"Crank."

A bolt of desire shoots through me at the sound of my name on her lips, needing and pleading. "Then I'm going to bring you to the edge, over and over and over while you scream for me."

Crash.

I swing the bathroom door closed behind me, making her yelp in surprise as she sits on the edge of the bathtub, her chest heaving, her eyes blown with desire as she stares at me.

Marching over, I twist my fingers into her hair and drag her to her feet, lowering my lips to her ear. "And then, when you can't take it anymore, I'm going to slide inside your tight pussy and fuck you until the only name you remember is mine."

She trembles in my hold, her dark eyes staring up into mine begging me for everything I've just described.

"You want that, sunshine?" I growl.

She nods.

"Not good enough. I want to hear it. I want to hear that you want me."

"I... I..." she hesitates and for a moment, I'm hit with the realization of her age.

Fuck.

Her eyes hold mine, narrowing as my panic hits.

I shouldn't be talking to her like this, standing

here naked before her, my cock weeping to have her lips wrapped around it again.

"I want it," she says, firmly this time. "I want this. Tonight. You."

"Fuck."

My lips slam down on hers, my arm banding around her waist, crushing her body to mine. She kisses me with the same intensity I do her, tongues dueling, teeth clashing, and my previous concern vanishes.

The differences between us don't matter when it's like this. We're just two people desperate for the other. Age is only a number.

My hands find the knot beneath her breasts and I damn near rip it open in my need to get her bare before me.

"Killian," she breathes as I pull the fabric from her shoulders, and fuck if hearing my real name doesn't do weird shit to me.

The club whores are all about the club and the only thing to ever fall from their lips is Crank. Hell, most of them don't even know my actual name. But hearing it falling from Quinn's lips is the most delicious kind of torture.

This right now is about more than the club, my status, and Quinn's need to be a part of something. Hell, she's actively trying to run away from it all. This is just us. Our need. Our burning heat.

"Oh God," she moans when I drag her bra from her body, my hands immediately cupping both her breasts, teasing her peaked nipples until she's panting into our kiss.

"Fuck, you're perfect. And all mine."

Lifting her, she wraps her legs around my waist, my cock brushing her soaked panties as I walk us from the bathroom, our lips never parting.

I press my knees to the edge of the bed and lay her down, finally breaking our kiss and trailing my lips across her jaw and down her neck, setting about driving her crazy just like I promised.

Her fingers twist in the hair at the nape of my neck as I bite and suck on her soft, sweet skin.

"You've got no idea how long I've dreamed about this," I murmur into the crook of her neck as I think about the first time I saw her in the Sinners' clubhouse all those weeks ago. I had no idea who she was, but fuck, she took my breath away.

Then when I learned the truth, I knew I needed to rid myself of my little obsession.

I told myself all the right things in an attempt to forget her.

She's their ex-VP's daughter. She's too young. Still in high school. Yet, despite all of that, I still fucking need her.

"Killian," she cries, her back arching off the bed as I suck her nipple into my mouth, swirling my tongue around the hard peak. "Oh God. Fuck."

"Jesus, sunshine," I groan, a smug grin playing on my lips as I move to the other side. "I could get you off just like this, huh?" I don't need her response, her body is telling me all I need to know.

She needs this almost as badly as I do.

"Please," she begs, making me chuckle.

"Have you forgotten what I said?" I ask, my voice rough with desire, my cock aching to slide deep inside her.

She shakes her head, her body moving with it as I tease her peak with the tip of my tongue.

"I'm going to bring you to the edge, over and over and over," I promise.

"Oh God," she whimpers.

"And I'm going to start here." I suck her once more, releasing her with a loud pop. "And then I'm going to spread your legs and eat you until the only thing you can think about is having my cock inside you."

"I'm there," she cries. "I'm already there. Please."

Chuckling against her full breast, I pinch the other. Hard. "You're nowhere near yet, sunshine," I tell her before diving for her once more, teasing her until her nails pierce the skin of my shoulders, the pain shooting straight to my cock.

"Fuck. Fuck. *Fuck*," she chants right before I sink my teeth into her nipple, making her scream.

She's so close, I can read it in every twitch of her body, every needy moan that rips from her lips.

Dropping down over her ribs, I lick a trail down her stomach, circling her belly button as my fingers tuck under the waistband of her skirt, dragging both that and her panties down her legs.

Standing at the foot of my bed, I discard her clothing and run my eyes from her feet and up every inch of her body. She's still wearing her cape, the sight makes a smile twitch at my lips. My filthy little superhero.

"Why are you laughing at me?" she snaps, a frown marring her brow.

"I'm not. I'm just..." I push my hand through my hair, dragging it back. "I've never seen anything more fuckin' perfect."

"Liar," she hisses. "You've had a million women right here."

"No," I tell her honestly, taking a step closer to her. "There's only one who's been in my bed. In this house. And she's exactly where she belongs."

Pressing my palms to her thighs, I spread her wide open for me as she gasps in shock, understanding the meaning behind my words.

This house is mine. My sanctuary. The only women who've been here before are my aunt and Kat. And now Quinn. My ray of sunshine.

Moonlight illuminates her glistening pussy and my mouth waters for another taste of her.

"W-what are you waiting for?" she breathes, noticing that I've stilled.

"Absolutely fuckin' nothing, sunshine."

Dropping to my stomach, I hold her legs as wide as they'll go and run the tip of my tongue from her entrance all the way up to her clit, letting her juices coat my tongue and her taste explode in my mouth.

Fucking heaven.

"Oh my God," she screams as I clamp my hands around her hips, holding her in place as I up my efforts on her clit, licking, sucking and nipping until she's crying out my name, fighting to get away from the intensity of my attack, but she can't move an inch.

Just before she's about to fall, I do exactly as I promised and pull back, doing nothing more than coating her swollen, heated skin with my heaving breaths.

"You're a fucking asshole, Killian Crankton."

A chuckle rumbles in my chest. "I'll be anything you want me to be, sunshine."

"I want you inside me, but you don't seem to be complying."

"Oh, baby. Trust me, I'm going to sink so deep inside you that you're going to see stars."

"Big words for a man who has yet to prove his worth."

My brow quirks. "Your juices are all over my face, sunshine. Your cunt is dripping for more. I'm pretty sure you're already aware of my worth."

"You're a fucking tease."

"Takes one to know one, baby. It's all you've been doing to me for weeks. I've spent way too much time jerking off to memories of you."

Moving my hand, I circle her entrance with one finger, halting whatever cutting reply was going to rip from her lips.

"I-I'm right here. Take it. Take me, please."

Moving my eyes up from her pussy, I take in her curves, her full breasts and pert nipples until I get to her dark, desire-filled, frustrated eyes.

"Quinn," I say, suddenly feeling sober from the high of her taste as a thought hits me. "Y-you're not a vir—"

Her tight grip on my hair cuts off my words. "Do I fucking look like it, Crankton?" she barks, forcefully dragging my face back between her legs.

"Okay," I chuckle, pushing two fingers deep inside her, bending them to find her G-spot.

"Holy fucking shit," she cries, her pussy sucking my fingers deeper as I latch onto her clit.

For the final time, I take her right to the edge.

The second I pull from her body, her head snaps up and she stares hate-filled daggers at me while I just smirk in response.

Crawling onto the bed, I shift between her thighs, rubbing the head of my cock through her wetness. She tilts her hips, trying to force me lower.

"You're wicked, sunshine."

"I'm desperate, that's what I am, asshole."

"Patience," I growl, leaning over her toward the nightstand to grab a condom.

Her chest heaves as she watches my every move, ripping open the little packet and rolling the rubber down my length. "You've got one last chance to change your mind, sunshine. Because once this happens, all bets are off," I warn her.

I had hoped that getting her to myself, finally getting inside her would get her out of my system. I'm not even inside her yet and I already know...

This is never going to be enough.

17

QUINN

Crank isn't gentle, his big hand grips my thigh and hooks my leg around his waist as he buries himself deep inside me.

I cry out right as he groans, a low gravelly sound that sends shivers through me.

"Fuck, you feel... fuckin' hell, sunshine." He holds still for a second and I revel in the feel of him. Thick and long, he fills and stretches me in a way that feels too damn good.

Too damn right.

Get those thoughts out of your head, Quinn.

This is one night.

Nothing more, nothing less.

"Move," I murmur, wrapping my arms around his broad shoulders, "I need you to move."

Crank pulls out slowly and pistons his hips forward, slamming back inside me.

"Shit, you're so tight. So fuckin' good." He

kisses me. Big open-mouthed kisses as if he's trying to devour me. Our tongues slide together, tasting and teasing as he rocks into me, fitting his body to mine as if he was born to do it.

God, this man is too much.

Too big.

Too skilled.

Too perfect.

And totally wrong for me.

So why does it feel so good?

Why does it feel like I've finally found what I've always been looking for, and just didn't realize?

"Never gonna let you go," he rasps against my lips, gripping my jaw and controlling the kiss, the same way he controls every roll and thrust of his hips.

I don't let his words wrap around my heart though, I can't. Not if I want to survive the aftermath of this.

Crank will tire of me eventually. He isn't the kind of guy that settles, he's the kind of guy that loves 'em and leaves 'em wanting more.

But I'm not that kind of girl.

Never have been and I'm not about to start now.

Not even for Killian and his magical fucking dick.

"Where'd you go just now?" His eyes bore into mine as he stills inside me once more.

"N-nowhere." I clench around him, trying to distract him.

"Fuck, do that again... milk my cock. Show me how much you want me."

"Crank," I whimper as he pulls out and slowly sinks back inside me.

"Don't call me that, not here. Not tonight."

"Killian." I press my palm to his cheek, grazing my lips over his. "Fuck me like the big bad biker I know you are."

A wicked smirk tugs at his lips. "Your wish is my command."

Without warning, he rocks back on his haunches and flips me over, pulling me back onto my knees. "Hold on," he demands, grabbing my hips and driving into me so hard I scream. "Fuck yeah." His pace is relentless, hard, punishing thrusts that make my back arch and breath catch.

Crank winds a hand into my hair and pulls my body up, latching his mouth onto my neck and sucking hard enough to break the skin.

"You're mine now, sunshine. This pussy, this body," his hands run all over my stomach and breasts, "that smart fuckin' mouth of yours, I want it all."

He cups my breasts, sucking on my neck as he rides my body, slow torturous strokes that drive me wild. I've never had sex like this before—sex with a man who knows exactly what he wants and how to get it.

His hand slips down my body, his fingers finding my clit and strumming in perfect synchrony with his brutal thrusts.

"God, Kill," I moan, breathless and ragged. "It feels..."

"I know, baby." He grabs my neck and tilts my head, kissing me deeply. "I know."

An intense wave of pleasure builds inside me, rising with every touch, every kiss, and stroke. Killian doesn't just fuck me... he completely consumes me.

He flips us again so I'm on top of him, riding him, slow and deep while his hands paint my body like a canvas. "Fuck, Quinn... fuckin' hell, yeah, like that, baby." He starts thrusting up into me until I shatter around him, crying his name like a prayer, over and over.

"I'm gonna come, I'm gonna... fuuuck." He fists my hair, dragging me down so we're face to face. His mouth crashes down on mine as he comes hard, jerking deep inside me. "Holy shit, sunshine." His lips curve against my mouth as he holds me there.

My heart races in my chest as the weight of what we've just done sinks into me.

"I should—"

"Hey," he says, touching his head to mine. "You good?"

I nod, not trusting myself to reply as I lie beside him, clutching the crumpled sheet to my body.

"Now she's shy." Crank chuckles, the sound reverberating through me.

"I need a girl's minute," I say, shifting to the edge of the bed.

He tucks his arm behind his head, watching me as I climb gingerly off the bed and scramble around to find my clothes. "You won't be needing those," he drawls, the heat in his voice a direct line to my core.

Jesus, he's trouble with a capital T, and I'm so screwed.

Literally and figuratively.

I slip into the small bathroom, flicking the light switch on this time. I'm surprised at how clean and tidy it is. Killian Crankton is an enigma I find myself wanting to understand. But that is never going to happen.

We're too different.

And this is... well, this is nothing more than a moment of madness. A stolen moment in time that we'll never get again.

The thought fills me with a strange sense of sadness, but I force it down. There's no use in getting attached to someone like Crank. He's the very definition of a player. I know he said that he's never brought a woman back here before, but it doesn't mean anything.

It isn't like he could risk taking me back to the clubhouse. If my dad finds out about this... A shudder rolls through me. It doesn't bear thinking about.

Bracing my hands against the sink, I stare at my reflection. I look the same—a little flushed and starry eyed—but I feel different. I feel like something changed tonight.

"What's taking you so long?" Crank appears, leaning against the doorjamb, his eyes searching mine in the mirror.

"Ever heard of privacy?" I snap.

He steps into the room and the air evaporates. "You look like you're ready to run again."

"I..."

The words die on my tongue as he reaches for me, wrapping his hand around my throat and turns me to face him. "Do I scare you, sunshine?" He leans in, brushing his lips over my jaw.

A whimper crawls up my throat but I swallow it.

"You're shaking." His other hand glides down my spine and presses on the small of my back, forcing us closer.

My hands go to his bare chest and I can't help but trace the ink decorating his skin.

"You like that?" he asks, and I find myself nodding.

It's like his voice hypnotizes me, pulling me deeper under his spell.

"Feel this." He takes one of my hands and

presses it to his rock hard dick. "That's what you do to me."

Power thrums in my veins, desire clouding my thoughts. I'm supposed to be leaving, walking away before I lose anymore of myself to him. But when Crank guides me into the shower, I don't protest. And when he pushes me up against the tiles, drops to his knees, and hooks my leg over his shoulder before burying his face in my pussy, I don't fight him.

Because the truth is, I want this.

I want everything he's willing to give me in this moment.

Consequences be damned.

I wake up plastered to a solid wall of heat. Crank's arm snakes over my hip, his possessive grip making my heart flutter. But panic quickly saturates my veins.

We fell asleep.

After he fucked me in the shower and again in his bed, we must have fallen asleep.

Crap.

I wriggle out of his hold, careful not to wake him and grab my cell phone.

A little before eight thirty.

Ugh.

How the hell am I going to explain this to the

girls? At least my parents think I'm sleeping over at Kat's house.

I glance over my shoulder, smiling at Killian as he sleeps. Dirty blond hair falls into his eyes making him look younger somehow, but his muscular inked body is testament to the man he is.

I can hardly drag my eyes off him, but I force myself to climb out of the bed and find my clothes, quickly pulling them on.

The last thing I want is to stick around for the awkward morning after. Neither of us talked about me staying over and I'm not going to be that girl.

Realizing that I can't leave his cabin in my Ginny Weasley costume, I search his dresser for a clean t-shirt and pull it over my body. It's too big, falling over my thighs but it's better than wandering around early in the morning looking like a sexy schoolgirl.

With one last look at Killian, I slip from his room and make my way downstairs. I have a couple of texts from Kat and River but nothing to suggest they were worried about me, which means they probably know where I am.

Or, at least, someone knows.

Great.

Just freakin' great.

I quickly text Kat back—begging her to come and get me—before making sure I've got everything then I leave Crank's cabin. I could wait inside for Kat to get here, but that would mean risking him waking up. And I'm not ready to see him again yet.

Last night needs to be filed away under a moment of weakness. It was good while it lasted but in the harsh light of day, it's something that can't ever happen again.

It was a bit of fun.

Nothing more.

So as I trudge toward the main road, why does it feel like I'm leaving a part of my heart behind?

18

CRANK

I wake with memories from the night before filling my mind. My body is hot as I remember exactly how hers felt writhing beneath me. My cock's hard as nails, desire filling my veins for another taste of the woman I already know I'm not going to be able to let go of.

It should terrify me. Any thoughts of needing a woman in the past always has. But Quinn. She's different. The only fear I feel right now is that I won't get to have her again.

I could try to convince myself that's because of last night. Of the sex. But I know it's more than that. That moment I pushed inside her and looked into her eyes.

Fuuuck.

She fucking ruined me in that moment.

So beautiful. So sexy. And so fucking mine.

My cock aches to feel it all over again, my

mouth waters to watch her fall over the edge, to see her skin flush as she comes with my name on her lips.

"Killian."

Shifting slightly, my heart drops when I don't immediately feel her pressed against me. But that's nothing compared to the sinking feeling that assaults me when I reach my hand out to find her and discover nothing more than an empty bed.

My head spins as I sit up, looking around the room for signs that she's not done exactly what I'm fearing she has. I scan the floor looking for her clothes but find none. Only open condom wrappers, the sight of that hits me like a ton of bricks and I fall back on to the bed, all the air rushing from my lungs.

I could go racing around the house in the hope that she's just in the kitchen making coffee, but I know it's just wishful thinking without even going to check. She's gone. I can feel it.

"Fuck," I roar, venting just a little of the frustration I feel.

It's what you've always wanted the woman to do in the past.

Irritated with myself, I throw the covers off and march straight into an ice-cold shower in the hope it both wakes me up and rids me of the images I really don't need in my head right now.

It's clear that she didn't wake up feeling the same.

You wanted to fuck her out of your system.

A bitter laugh rips from my lips as I press my palms against the cool tiles and hang my head.

She walked out. After everything... she just fucking walked out.

My fists curl, anger surging through me once again.

You're a fucking idiot, Killian Crankton.

The second I step back into my bedroom, I know that I need to get out of the fucking house. It smells like her. And sex.

Dragging on a clean pair of jeans and a shirt, I go in search of my cut and a cup of very strong coffee before disappearing out of the house, wishing I could leave the memories and the ache in my chest I'm trying desperately hard to ignore, behind.

The cabin through the trees where last night's party was looks like it was hit by a small hurricane. There are bodies littered around, decorations are flapping in the wind and there are bottles and Solo cups everywhere.

"Hey, Bones," I bark, none too gently kicking him in the stomach. "Get the fuck up and either help me or fuck off."

He groans, rolling over and immediately passing back out.

I do the same to another few guys, none of which actually wake up or listen to me. I understand why when I look at my cell and discover that it's barely even ten. I bet the party has literally only just stopped.

Stepping into the building, I assess the devastation. It's the same every year, which is why we always hire a clean up team to come later on in the day.

Stepping over a couple of people, I make my way to the bar, kicking a bottle out of the way as I go, ensuring it clatters against the wall with a loud crash, earning me more than a few groans of irritation.

Hopping up on one of the stools, I place my coffee on the bar and wrap my hands around it, letting the heat soothe me. Loud snores and grunts fill the space, but it's a hell of a lot better than the silence of my house.

I'm still sitting there, drowning in my own shitty decisions when a rumble of an engine hits my ears. I don't move, knowing that whoever it is will find me eventually.

"Oh hey, I wasn't expecting to find anyone alive here yet," a familiar voice says.

Letting out a sigh, I spin around on the stool and meet Dane's eyes.

"Oh shit, what happened?" he asks the second he registers the anger on my face.

"Nothing I wanna talk about," I snap, finally jumping up and setting about collecting up some of the bottles.

"What are you doing?"

I shrug.

"We've got people coming to do that, right?" Dane asks, his eyes tracking my every movement.

"I need to do something."

He chuckles behind me, and it makes my blood boil.

"You think this is fuckin' funny?" I bark, spinning toward him and taking a threatening step forward.

He doesn't so much as flinch. "I don't know you all that well yet, Crank. But yeah, watching you get whipped is quite amusing."

My jaw ticks as a smirk curls at his lips. "I get it, man," he says. "Sadie's got my balls firmly in her grasp. Only difference is, I handed mine over willingly."

My lips part to argue but I soon find I have no response.

"Wanna talk about it?" he offers.

"Do I fuckin' look like I wanna talk about it?" I bark, storming off toward the back of the room.

"I could really do with a coffee," he mutters, moving around behind me. "I also hear you've got a pretty sweet deck that looks out over the lake."

"Who told you that?" I ask, my heart jumping into my throat. Hardly any of the guys have ever been to my place. Dev used to hang out here with me, but other than that, we pretty much spend all our time at the clubhouse. My cabin is my escape.

The only other person who...

"Diesel," I conclude. "That motherfucker needs to keep his fuckin' nose out of my business."

Dane just stares at me, allowing me to rant.

"So... coffee?"

"Fuckin' hell," I mutter, storming past him and leading the way through the trees, knowing without looking back that he's following me.

"Whoa, I never had you down for a cabin in the woods kinda guy," he mutters behind me as my house comes into view.

"I like to hide sometimes."

"Well, it's the perfect place. I could see the four of us somewhere in a place like this. Peace and quiet, plenty of outside space to have se—" I turn around and raise a brow at him.

I can't help but laugh when all he does is shrug and say, "Don't tell me you've never wanted to do it against one of these trees. Or in the lake."

"Honestly, no. I've never brought a woman back here."

"So last night you didn't..."

"You fuckin' coming in or what?" I snap, continuing forward and pushing through my front door.

I keep my eyes focused on my kitchen, trying to keep images of having Quinn on her knees before me in here out of my head.

"This place is really fucking sweet, man," Dane says, sitting back in one of the chairs on my deck, looking out over the lake.

"Yeah, it's not bad."

"Go on then," he prompts.

"Nothin' to talk about."

"You know that Sadie and Quinn are tight, right? We know she was here last night, man."

Scrubbing my hand down my face, I focus on the ripple of the water before me. "I made a mistake," I confess.

"That gonna be your starting line with Micky?"

My heart slams in my chest. "Fuck... I— Shit."

"She that bad? I know she can be an uptight bi—"

My eyes shoot to his and he immediately shuts up, reading the warning loud and clear in my expression as my jaw ticks and my teeth grind.

"She's not as fun-loving as Sadie... at times. But I thought once you got your hands on her..."

Shaking my head, I rest back once more. "It was... It was fuckin' insane, man. She... she's like no woman I've ever met before. She makes me think all this shit I have no business thinking about, especially when it comes to her. I just... I dunno what the fuck I'm doing." I slam my lips shut the second I realize everything I'm thinking just fell out of my mouth.

"She's got right under your skin, huh?"

"I thought if I fucked her then... I dunno, I'd be able to put her behind me with all the others and move on. I've got no place thinking the things I do about her. She's in fuckin' high school, man."

"So am I, but you don't seem to have an issue with that."

I quirk a brow at him. "I don't want to fuck you six ways from Sunday."

"Well that's good. I've got enough on my plate. Not sure I've got the energy for anymore." He winks.

"Sadie just that good, huh?"

"Bro, you've no fucking idea." There's a wicked twinkle in his eyes that shoots all kinds of jealousy through my veins.

He makes it all look so easy. The four of them have a completely unconventional set up going on yet, they make it look so natural. So normal.

"Doesn't it terrify you?"

"What? Fucking the same insanely hot woman for the rest of my life? No, can't say that doesn't bother me in the slightest."

A smile curls at my lips. The thought of only ever having Quinn beneath me isn't freaking me out like it probably should. But that's not what I meant.

"No, I mean, this life. Committing to someone when..."

"We do all this shit," he says, throwing his arms out.

"Yeah. I've lost... too many fuckin' people. The fact I'm still here is a miracle after... yeah," I trail off. Dane doesn't need me bringing all that shit with his brother up.

"Life's too short not to try, don't you think?" he asks, spinning my words on their head and coming at it from another angle. "If I died tomorrow, I'd go a very, very happy man."

"But you'd leave her—"

"Sadie is a fighter. She knows the deal. She's lived this life just as long as we have. Quinn too."

"Quinn's not interested in this life though," I say, my voice conveying just how that statement makes me feel.

"She thinks she doesn't. But the club runs through her veins just like it does the rest of us. She might just need a *poke* in the right direction," he suggests.

"Fuckin' hell, bro."

"What?" he asks innocently sipping on his coffee. "So you dragged her off last night and what? Told her a bedtime story and tucked her in?"

I sit back, tugging at my jeans as thoughts of what really happened last night threaten to consume me. "Something like that. Clearly didn't impress her, she was gone before I woke up this morning."

Sitting forward, Dane scrubs his hand down his face, looking at me through sympathetic eyes. "Did you ever think that maybe she did that for you?"

"How the fuck would her sneaking out have been for me?"

"Because she probably thought it was what you wanted? You've got a rep, Crank. She knows what your MO is. She's just toeing the line. Being what you expect."

My chin drops. "But I didn't—"

"No point telling me that, bro. Maybe you should tell her?"

"Fuck," I hiss. "Fuck. Fuck."

Dane sits back with a smug ass smile playing on his lips.

"See, this is why I'm the boss."

19

QUINN

"So let me get this straight," Kat says quietly. "Crank chased you through the woods to his place and then you guys—"

"Don't." I lunge for her, clapping my hand over her mouth. "Don't say it."

We both fall back onto her bed, her laughter doing little to ease the huge knot in my stomach. The one that's been there ever since I fled his cabin earlier.

Kat picked me up and we came back to her house but instead of owning up to what really happened, I asked if I could crash for a while.

There's no escaping her third degree now though.

"Was he good?" Her brows knit. "Actually, don't answer that, it's weird. He's like my brother."

"It doesn't matter," I say, staring up at the ceiling, trying hard to forget what it felt like to be under him. On top of him. On my knees before him.

God, he really left a mark on my soul. A stain I'm not sure I'll ever scrub clean.

It was supposed to be just sex. One night of reckless abandon.

Instead, I've done nothing but think about him. The way he held me, kissed, and touched me. It was more than just sex even if my heart knows it's foolish to let my head go there.

Killian is older than me—too old—and we're too different. I want to go to college and see the world and get out of Savage Falls. He's all about the club, family and small town life.

It could never work... even if I wanted it too.

And I don't.

"I think it does." She turns to look at me, but I don't meet her piercing stare. "I think you like him."

"Crank is..."

"Ridiculously hot. Loyal. Solid. Did I mention hot?" She nudges my shoulder, chuckling.

"It was... intense." I admit, finally meeting her gaze.

"Intense how?"

"I don't know." My shoulders lift in a small shrug. "I've never been with a guy like Crank. Maybe it's just an older guy thing."

"Or maybe he got you on a sexual level that other guys you've been with never have."

"Maybe." The thought strikes a chord with me. Jake was nice, and the sex was okay. But it wasn't earth-shattering. He didn't make me feel like the center of his universe. He didn't know exactly how to touch me or talk dirty in my ear to make me fall apart.

I'd be lying if I said I didn't like Crank's dirty mouth, his arrogant confidence.

This is a disaster.

One night of sex and I've caught feelings, exactly the opposite of what was supposed to happen.

What did I really expect though?

I don't have meaningless one-night stands, I've never really been that kind of girl. I'm the total opposite of the kind of girl Crank goes for, so why me?

Why did he insist on taking me to his cabin? Why did he say all of those things to me?

"Want to know what I think?" Kat grins.

"Not really."

"Tough shit. I think the two of you have something going on, something that scares you both."

"Crank doesn't like me, Kat. I'm eighteen, still in high school. He's used to women like Lucy, women who—"

"Exactly. You're everything he's never allowed himself to want. Smart. Gorgeous. Someone who knows what the club means, understands the sacrifice it can require. Lucy and the rest of the club whores might think they know, but they don't. How could they?"

Her expression sobers and I squeeze her hand. Diesel wasn't injured in the recent war with Darren Creed and the rogue Reapers, but they still lost a lot of good men. Men she knew.

"I want more, Kat." My voice cracks but it's the truth. I've always wanted more than a life in Savage Falls, a life in the club.

"I'm not suggesting you have to marry the guy and have his babies. But what if he's your person?"

"My person?" I shake my head. "Crank is not my person."

"Okay." She sits up and folds her legs. "Let me put it like this... would you be really okay with never seeing him again? Never speaking to him or—"

"Stop," I sigh. "Please just stop. It was one night, Kat. That's all it'll ever be."

"Fine." She doesn't look convinced. "I won't mention it again. But I will say this. Killian is a good man, Quinn. Sure, he's a bit of a player. What single good-looking guy isn't? But he never leads them on, and he always calls it off if things get messy. And ever since I've been old enough to know what guys like my brother and Crank like to do with women behind closed doors, I've never known him to take anyone who isn't family out to his cabin."

"Are you done?" My brow quirks in irritation.

But it isn't Kat I'm irritated with, not really.

I'm irritated at myself for ever getting into this situation.

Because she's right.

Of course she's right, I just don't need to hear about how good Killian is. Not when I'm trying my hardest to push him to the recess of my mind.

"Yeah, I'm done."

"Good, I guess I should think about going home."

"Are you going to tell your mom and dad where you were all night?" She smirks.

"Have you lost your freaking mind? No, I'm not going to tell them. The club is finally getting things straight, I don't want my dad to cause any more drama."

"You really think he'd care?"

"I'm his daughter, his eighteen-year-old daughter, of course he'd care."

"Sadie's only eighteen but Ray was cool about her and the guys."

"It's not the same. Sadie is... she's always been a free spirit who enjoys pushing the boundaries. Ray went along with it because he knew it was a battle he wouldn't win. Once she sets her mind on something..."

"Yeah, I can see that."

I sit up and release a steady breath. "I really appreciate you letting me crash here today."

"Any time. It's nice having another girl around."

"I still can't believe River had to go home. I hope she's okay."

Kat stands and grabs her keys off her desk. "She drank a lot."

"She did?" That doesn't sound like River.

"Yeah, after we did the scare house, she was like a girl on a mission. I could hardly keep up with her."

"Did she say anything?"

"No, why?"

"Just doesn't sound like her." I shrug, making a mental note to talk to River.

I know she was upset over Jax showing his true colors, but getting wasted at a party isn't her MO. Not unless something happened.

"We all need to cut loose once in a while. It's just a good thing Rhett was there to take her home. Come on, I'll give you a ride."

We leave the house right as Diesel pulls into the driveway on his bike.

"Didn't expect to see you here," he says, eyeing me with a knowing smirk.

My cheeks burn as I murmur something about being hungover and hurry to get into Kat's car.

The two of them share a heated discussion. Diesel rolls his eyes, glancing in my direction. Kat climbs into the driver's side a second later, slamming the door behind her.

"Everything okay?" I ask.

"Yup." She snaps, jamming her key in the ignition. "Just my brother being his usual asshole self."

"Oh," I say, staring out of the window, unable to shake the feeling that they weren't just having a sibling spat...

That, maybe, they were talking about me.

"Hey, Mom," I call out as I enter the house.

Kat never said anything more about her conversation with Diesel, and I didn't ask.

Last night was a one-time thing—something I need to file away under 'never going to happen again.'

Crank is exactly the kind of guy I need to stay away from, and I'm exactly the kind of girl he doesn't want.

"In the kitchen, sweetheart."

I follow the smell of freshly baked cookies, my stomach groaning at the rack of baked goods. "Hmm, something smells good."

"They're just cooling. How was the party?"

"It was good." I nod, avoiding eye contact. "Where's Dad?"

"He's over in Red Ridge. Got a feeling he'll be there a lot, helps him feel useful." Sadness washes over her.

"It's going to take time, Mom."

"I know, sweetheart, I know. I'm just glad he's out and about instead of sitting in that damn chair all day. He needs to keep his brain active."

"And what about you?" I ask.

"Oh, you know me, sweetie. I'll be okay. So, tell me everything. How was your date?"

Oh God.

Trent.

I haven't even thought twice about him. The last I saw, he was getting up close and personal with Lucy, of all people. And I have a sneaky suspicion that was all a set up to push me and Crank together.

"What?" Mom asks, and I blink at her.

"Nothing. You know, it wasn't really a date, it was... just a friend thing."

"One day, sweetheart. One day, you'll meet the guy who makes your heart flutter and your pulse race. I knew the second I laid eyes on your daddy that he was the guy for me."

"Come on, Mom. It doesn't happen like that."

"Says who?" She chuckles softly. "Society? God? I don't need anyone to tell me what I feel or whether it's right or wrong. Trust your heart, sweetheart, I always have and it's never steered me wrong."

She makes it sound so simple, when in reality it's anything but.

"I'm still young, Mom. There's plenty of time

to meet guys and date and all of that other stuff."
As I say the words, my stomach turns.

Is that what I really want? To date guy after
guy waiting for that magical spark? Hoping to find
a connection with someone that burns brighter
than what I experience whenever Crank's around?

Images flood my mind of last night. Our bodies
pressed together, mouths and teeth and tongues.
Skin on skin. Hands touching and bodies moving.

It really was like nothing I've ever felt before.

But it was just because he's older, more
experienced. Not because there's some kind of
soulmate connection between us.

I don't even know if I believe in soulmates for
Christ's sake.

The front door rattles and Dad's gruff voice fills
the house. "Dee, baby, a little help."

She comes around and drops a kiss on my
head before disappearing down the hall. I snag a
cookie and tear off a piece, popping it in my
mouth. Seconds later, I hear the telltale whoosh
of my dad's chair, and turn to find him watching
me.

"Hey, Daddy." I climb off the stool and go to
him, but his expression is cold. "D-Daddy?" I choke
out, feeling the walls begin to close in on me.

He knows... my dad knows about last night.

"I can explain," I rush out. "I was—"

Voices out in the hall catch my attention, and I
look past my father.

"Crank gave your daddy a ride home." Mom appears, smiling. "Isn't that nice of him?"

"Nice... yeah." My throat is dry, my heart galloping in my chest.

He told him.

He told my dad about what happened.

That sneaky traitorous piece of shit.

"Quinn," Crank says curtly.

"Quinn," I murmur to myself. "You have got to be kidding me."

"Sweetheart?" Mom glances between the two of us. "Is everything okay?"

"Everything is fine, Mom." I level Crank with a cold stare. "Everything is just fine."

What I really want to do is leap across the room and strangle him. Why the hell would he do this to me? The last person who ever needed to know about last night was my father. What the hell was he thinking?

"Daddy, I can explain..."

"Crank explained everything well enough," he replies with a thin expression.

"H-he did?"

"Yes, he did. Now why don't we all sit and discuss this, like adults."

"Micky?" Mom asks, confusion etched onto her face.

"Let's sit, Dee. Crank has some rather interesting things to tell you."

Oh God... this is happening.

It's actually happening.

I want the ground to open up and swallow me whole.

"Daddy, we should discuss this as a family. Crank doesn't need to be here." I shoot him another hard look, but his stone mask gives little away.

"Of course he needs to be here." He lets out a heavy sigh. "Let's just get this over with."

Over with?

My gaze snaps to Killian who doesn't show even an ounce of remorse.

What the hell did he tell him?

20

CRANK

My cell ringing cuts off anything else Dane has to say about the Quinn situation, although really, his smug grin says it all.

He knows he's right. Dammit.

Pulling my cell out, my heart drops into my feet when I find Micky's name staring back at me.

"What is it?" Dane asks, seeing my expression change.

"Micky."

He throws his head back and laughs, much to my irritation. "You really think she went running home and told daddy everything you did to her? Bro, come on. This is Quinn, not a club whore. She's not going to be bragging to everyone who'll listen, especially to her old man."

I hold his eyes for a beat as my cell continues to ring.

"Answer it. Unless you're planning on being a

pussy, going nomad and running from all of this."
His brow lifts and I swipe my screen and bring my
cell to my ear.

"Crank."

"You coming in, son? I'm going through the
accounts and... well..."

"Yeah, I'll be there in about thirty."

He hangs up before I get the chance. Micky's
never been one with words, but still, that was a bit
cold, and does little to alleviate my anxiety over
him finding out.

"Looks like we're making a move," I tell Dane.

"I was heading there next anyway. Need to see
if you've run my club into the ground."

"Building back from the ground up, man.
We've still got a lot of work to do, but the Sinners
might just have saved it."

"This club isn't the only one," he mutters.

"We're gonna make this work, Prez," I say with
fierce determination in my voice as I slide to the
edge of the chair. "Things aren't gonna be easy, but
we're going to make something epic. I can feel it."

Slowly, he begins to nod. "Yeah, we are. I've got
a good feeling about all this."

"Come on then, we need to go and look at our
accounts. They don't sound pretty."

"Wow, you know how to bring all the fun," he
mutters, trailing me into the house. "You gonna talk
to Micky?"

I freeze and he laughs.

"You want her Crank, you're gonna have to pull out the big guns."

The second we arrived at the compound, Dane and I went straight to his office and found Micky knee deep in invoices and receipts.

We'd been focusing on getting the shop back up and running so we could have some money coming back in, we hadn't even touched the accounts, which it seems could have been a mistake.

By the time we've got everything into some kind of order and more or less aware of where the shop stood financially, my eyes were beginning to cross, and it was obvious that Micky was struggling.

He likes to pretend that he didn't almost die only a few weeks ago, but some days the exhaustion is clear as day in his features.

"Crank, why don't you take Micky home?" Dane suggests after we've emerged from the office and grabbed a couple of drinks from the bar.

"Uh..." I glance at the man himself and guilt tugs at me when I take in his dark eyes and pale complexion.

"Yeah, sure thing," I say, forcing down our impending conversation.

Dane is right. If I want us to stand any chance, then I need to do the right thing, And that means talking to Micky. It means being honest about what I really want, even if it terrifies me.

"Come on, old man. Let's get you home," I say, much to his irritation, although he's too exhausted to actually fight me on it.

Right before we step out of the clubhouse, a strong hand clamps down on my shoulder. "There's nothing wrong with going after something you want, man. Even if it's different."

I nod at Dane's advice and continue pushing Micky toward the truck and helping him inside.

"We're not going anywhere, son," Micky points out a few minutes after I've started the engine but made no move to actually leave.

I stare straight ahead at the building before us and suck in a deep breath. "I need to talk to you," I say before I change my mind.

"Oh?"

"Yeah... I, um..." *Shit.*

Pushing my hair back from my brow, I try to figure out how to say what I need to say without me ending up being castrated by Quinn's father.

"I wanted to ask your permission to date your daughter."

Micky damn near chokes on his own breath as my words hit him. "You want to *date* my daughter?" he asks, his voice cold, hard, and devoid of any emotion.

"Uh... yeah. I really like her, sir, but I don't

want to go behind your back." More than I already have.

The tension in the car is almost unbearable, the air suffocating.

"And you think she wants the same?"

I can't help but laugh at his question. "No. I'm still trying to convince her that it's a good idea."

"Smart girl," he mutters, scrubbing his hand over his rough chin.

"Yeah, smarter than me," I agree. "But I really like her. She's... fuck, I don't know. Just being with her, it's..." I relax a little, thinking of all the time I've spent with her. Even if it has been arguing and exchanging cutting remarks. She's like no one I've ever spent time with before. She challenges me in a way I've never experienced and makes me want things I've never considered an option for me.

Silence stretches out between us and my palms start to sweat against the wheel.

He's going to say no, I know he is. And then where does that leave me?

I'm trying to do the right thing here, Micky, I silently plead.

"Quinn isn't interested in this life, Crank. No matter what I've done to include her, she's pushed against me at every turn." A heavy sigh escapes his lips. "She wants college, a life outside of Savage Falls and MCs."

"I know, and I want her to have that too, if it's what she wants. I'd never try to stop her."

His lips part, and I can almost hear the question that's on the tip of his tongue.

But how would that work?

I have no fucking clue. It might not. But fuck if I don't want to at least try.

"Are you taking me home then or what?" he barks when it becomes clear that I've got no intention of moving any time soon.

So without an answer, and with my heart still slamming against my ribs, I back out of the space and head toward Savage Falls.

No words are said between us all the way back, and as we approach their house, I swear I actually stop breathing.

The sight of Quinn's car sitting in the driveway sure doesn't help the situation.

I come to a stop and wait for him to get out. But he hesitates while the engine continues to run. "I guess you'd better come in then."

He's pushed his door open and swung his legs out before his words have registered.

"Shit, yeah. Okay."

I've got him in his chair and we're at the front door before he speaks again.

"Like I said, my daughter is a smart girl. And you seem to think she's mature enough for a man like you so we'll see what she thinks about all of this, shall we?"

I swallow nervously as I swing the front door open and push him inside.

Dee is immediately there to help, a kind, soft smile playing on her lips as she thanks me for delivering Micky home safely.

"Crank actually needs to come in. We've all got some things to discuss," Micky tells his old lady, his voice giving nothing away.

"Okay." She frowns. "Well, come on in, Crank. You're more than welcome in our house."

We'll see.

With concern filling her eyes, Dee gestures for me to walk further inside.

The second I hear Quinn's voice as she says hello to her father, it does something to me, something that tells me what I'm doing is right.

Although when her eyes fall on me, it's clear she doesn't feel the same way.

Only ten minutes later, the four of us are sitting around the dining table each with a coffee and freshly baked cookies. Quinn looks like she's about to explode, Micky is still as unreadable as he was in the truck and Dee is just confused as she lowers herself beside me.

"What is it, Crank? You two have me all worried."

Micky scoffs and Quinn damn near trembles with anger opposite me.

Throwing my shoulders back, I come straight out with it. "I want to know if I have both of your permission to date your daughter."

Dee's chin drops, a weird, half-amused half-shocked noise falls from her lips.

But if Quinn is shocked, then she doesn't show it because all that comes from her is pure fury. "Are you actually serious right now? You're here to ask for permission. What am I? A child?"

"Sweetheart, that's not what Crank is trying to imply," Dee says, quickly adding, "or I severely hope not."

"I'm tryin' to do this the right way, Quinn. I like you. I've made no secret of that fact. I want to spend more time with you, and I don't want that time to be sneaking around scared of what your father might do when he finds out."

Micky grunts but that's as much of a reaction as I get out of him. I've got no fucking clue where his head is at with all this.

"That's really good of you, Crank. We appreciate you being a gentleman about this."

I fight the need to think back to just how much of a gentleman I was last night, but when I catch Quinn's burning stare the memories come back faster than I can control.

"I know you're not going to be overly happy about this. But I really want—"

"Enough," Quinn snaps, jumping up so fast her chair topples behind her. "You need to leave. I'm not doing this, Crank. You don't get to storm in here and try to take exactly what you want."

"Quinn," I breathe. "That's the opposite of

what I'm tryin' to do." I push my hair back, exasperated with the fact I can't seem to do anything right when it comes to her.

"I don't care. I don't fucking care. You can't do this."

She's gone before I get a chance to call her back. All three of us watch her escape before the sound of a slamming door rattles through the house.

"Changed your mind yet?" Micky mutters, speaking for the first time in what feels like forever.

"I ambushed her." *He* ambushed her. I never would have done it like this if I had my way. I just wanted to talk to him, hopefully get his permission and then figure out a way forward. "I should go, give you guys some space."

Pushing to stand, I take a step away but stop at the sound of Dee's voice.

"We appreciate what you've done, Crank. I can't imagine talking to him," she shoots her husband an amused glance, "about any of this was easy. But we trust our daughter, Crank. If she thinks you're worthy of her time, then we can only follow her lead."

"T-thank you, Dee."

Looking over to Micky, he nods. "Should not change your mind after this, just treat her right, and we won't have an issue."

"You got it. I'll let her cool off."

"I'll talk to her. You're a good boy, Crank. She'd be an idiot not to see it."

With one more smile at Dee and a nod in Micky's direction, I take off, leaving Quinn behind.

It's the last thing I want to do, but I know I need to.

I don't bother going back to the compound, instead, I take the truck straight back to my cabin. I need the peace and quiet after that.

Part of me thinks I handled it wrong, but then dragging Quinn into the whole thing wasn't part of my plan. I just wanted to talk to Micky.

Grabbing a couple of beers from the fridge, I make my way down to the end of my jetty that hangs out over the lake and take a seat with my legs dangling over the edge.

Silence surrounds me and I lose myself in my thoughts.

I've got no idea how long I sit there, but my beers are gone and the sun is quickly sinking behind the trees that surround the lake when the rustle of leaves alert me to someone approaching.

Sucking in a deep breath as I prepare to turn around and find either Diesel or Dane.

But my eyes land on a very different person and I hop to my feet as she closes the distance between us.

21

QUINN

"Why?" The word falls from my lips as I stare at Crank.

I've spent the last couple hours trying to process his words. I should be elated that he came for me, that he proved me wrong. But all I feel is gnawing torment. This has to be a joke. Some kind of sick joke to get me to fall at his feet so he can kick me to the curb when he's done playing with me.

Isn't it?

I ignore the little voice trying to get me to give him a chance. If I give Killian a chance all I'll get is a broken heart. I'd be stupid to even contemplate it...

And yet, he came for me.

He asked my parents for their blessing.

"You want me to get on my knees and beg, sunshine? Because I will."

"No, I don't want you to beg. I want to know

why? You don't date. You don't ask parents for their permission to date their daughters... I just don't understand—"

"It's all you, Quinn. You knocked me on my ass the first time I laid eyes on you. Couldn't get you out of my fuckin' head..." he reaches for me, sliding his hand up the side of my neck. "Knew I'd go out of my mind if I didn't get a chance to taste your pussy."

"Crank..." Heat floods me but I keep my expression neutral. I can't fall under his spell again, not while we're having this conversation.

"I like sex," he says with a small smirk. "I like sex without strings. Always have—"

"I swear to God, if you finish that sentence, I will knee you in the balls."

"If you let me finish, I was going to say that... I like sex with you more." He leans in, dropping his head to mine. My fingers curl into his tank top.

"Keep talking." A faint smile plays on my lips.

"You're different, Quinn. Like no one I've ever met. And I don't want to scare you off before I've ever got you, but being around you makes me think about things I've never given much thought to before."

A thrill goes through me, my heart fluttering wildly in my chest.

"You like me," I whisper.

"Baby, I'm fuckin' crazy about you. And after last night—I'm still pissed at the fact you ran out on me, by the way—it only cemented things for me." He dips his face to look me dead in the eye. "There's something between us, sunshine. And I want to explore it."

"I'm a senior, Crank." I sigh. "I'm going to college next fall. I want to travel, I want—"

"I want you to have all those things, baby." His lips hover precariously close to mine. "I want you to fly high and free. I just want you to always come back to me."

"Y-you do?"

"Yeah, I do."

He might as well have reached inside my chest and fisted my heart.

"I got your parents' blessing... I guess all I need now is yours."

God, he looks at me with so much hope and vulnerability, it cracks my chest wide open.

This big bad biker is laying it all out on the line... for me. Suddenly, it feels like too much pressure to hold his heart in the palm of my hand.

"I..." I press my lips together, unsure of what words will escape if I let them.

"You, Quinn. It's you," he breathes the words against my lips, and a whimper crawls up my throat.

"Just give me a chance, sunshine. Let me be the kinda guy you deserve."

He's wrong for me.

Everything I've wanted to get away from.

He wraps me up in his arms. Damn, why does it feel like I'm exactly where I'm supposed to be?

"If we do this..." My voice trembles. "I won't sit by and watch you with anyone else, Crank. I won't be that girl."

"Never gonna happen. Your pussy's got me all kinds of addicted."

"Can you be serious for a second?" I quirk a brow and he chuckles.

"I am serious. I want you in my bed and on the back of my bike. I—"

"Whoa, on the back of your bike? That's a little more than dating, Crank."

"Killian." He ghosts his mouth over mine. "When it's just the two of us together, I'm Killian."

"If we do this... we need to take it slow."

"Slow, got it." His eyes dance with amusement.

I turn to swat at his chest. "I mean it, Kill. You... you scare me."

Hurt flashes in his eyes as he jerks back like I've slapped him. "I scare you?"

"No, that's... that came out wrong." I sigh. "I just mean, the way you make me feel. The way I feel around you... that scares me. You're a biker—"

He curves a hand around the back of my neck and draws me close again. "I'm your biker, sunshine."

"Mine, huh?" I fight a grin.

"Yeah." He grins back, and something snaps into place between us. "If you'll have me."

"I'll have to think about it." I tease, surprised at how natural this feels.

"She'll think about it," he murmurs.

I grab his cut and yank him closer. "I'm sure there's something you can do to persuade me."

His eyes light up. "I can think of a couple of things. But first, I'm hungry." He scoops me up and throws me over his shoulder.

"Kill, put me down! Put me the hell—"

The crack of his hand across my ass startles me.

"You did not just do that."

"You're all mine now, sunshine." He takes off toward the stairs. "And I need to eat."

Heat curls in my stomach. "You need to eat, huh? And what exactly is it you plan on eating?"

His voice is a rough whisper as he chuckles.

"You."

"Again?" I pant, my legs like jelly as he pulls them over his shoulders and buries his face in my pussy.

"Still hungry," he grumbles, the vibrations sending sparks of pleasure shooting through me.

"God, Kill." My fingers twist into his hair as he spears his tongue deep inside me, sliding fingers over my clit with skilled precision. I arch off the bed, locking my legs around him.

I've lost count of how many times he's made me

come since I turned up here earlier. It's like he can't get enough of me.

I'm exhausted. Sated and spent. But he's obviously taking his mission of persuading me very very seriously.

"Taste so fuckin' good." He lifts his head and smirks at me, pushing two fingers deep inside me, stretching me. His body rocks gently and I push up on my elbows and frown.

"Are you jacking off?"

A sexy smirk traces his mouth. "I've got my fingers in your pussy and your taste on my tongue. Fuck yeah, I'm jacking off." He groans and my pussy gushes around him.

"You like that, sunshine? You like it when I talk dirty."

I do.

I really do.

"I'm close." It comes out breathy as he works me faster.

"Fuck yeah." He dives at me again, lapping and sucking, flicking his tongue over my clit and grazing it with his teeth. My body is a storm of sensation as Killian makes me come apart, touch by touch.

"More... oh God," I cry, writhing against him.

"Never gonna get enough of this." He pushes another finger into me and curls them.

Pleasure barrels into me and I scream his name, riding out the intense waves of pleasure. He kisses the inside of my thigh before rising over my body and fisting his cock.

"Need to mark you," he groans as hot jets of cum land on my chest and stomach. Reaching down, he smears his fingers through the sticky mess, painting his name across my breasts. "Much better."

"You are so dirty."

"But you love it... you do love it, right?" A flash of uncertainty fills his expression.

"Yeah." I smile. "I love it."

"Thank fuck." He flops down beside me, tucking me under his arm. "You know when I woke up this morning and realized you ran, I was pissed. For the first time in my life, I cared. I know you want to go slow but I've never been one to shy away from the hard things in life. So you need to know that I'm in, sunshine. I'm all fuckin' in."

"You are, huh?" I crane my neck to look at him.

"I am. Doesn't mean that I want to clip your wings, I don't. I know you're still young. I know you have things you wanna do. But I want to be the guy at your side. I want to be the guy you come home to."

Who knew Killian Crankton could be such a romantic?

"You really think we can make this work?" I ask.

"I know we can. You just got to give me a chance, Quinn."

I gaze at him, already knowing my answer. But it won't hurt to make him suffer a little while longer. "I don't know." I smirk. "You should probably work on persuading me a little more."

A deep laugh rumbles in his chest as he rolls on top of me, not caring that I'm covered in his cum.

"You want my cock, sunshine?" He teases the tip against my entrance, slowly inching inside me. "You only have to ask."

The Red Ridge compound comes into view and I grip Killian's waist tighter. I can't believe he already got me on the back of his bike. But as I've learned, he can be very persuasive, as I spent the day discovering in many different ways.

I wasn't sure when he asked me to come with him. But he seemed so excited to tell the guys our news that I didn't want to burst his bubble.

So here I am. On the back of his bike, breaking every rule I've ever had for myself.

He pulls up outside the shop and kills the engine. I slide off the bike and he gently pulls the helmet off my head. "Ready?" he asks.

"As I'll ever be."

"You're my woman now, Quinn. You don't ever have to worry about coming around here."

Because he's VP.

I'm with the VP of the Red Ridge Sinners.

Oh God.

How the hell did I end up here?

The urge to run floods my veins, but I stand my ground.

He's right. We need to get this over with. The sooner people know, the sooner they'll get used to it.

The sooner I'll get used to it.

He climbs off his bike and takes my hand in his as if it's the most natural thing in the world. A couple of guys working in the shop glance our way but keep their thoughts to themselves.

"Come on." He pulls me toward the clubhouse.

The second we step inside, the whole place falls silent, every pair of eyes home in on our joined hands.

"Well, fuck me," someone bellows. "Looks like the VP went and got himself an old lady."

I flinch at the words.

Old lady... dear God.

"Listen up," Killian shouts. "For those of you who don't know, this here is Quinn, Micky's daughter."

"You tapping that, Crank?" Another guy hollers and a ripple goes through the air. Killian rips his hand away from me and storms toward the guy in question.

Grabbing him by the throat, he slams him against the wall and gets right up in his face. "Quinn is my girl. Anyone got a problem with that they can see me about it. That goes for all of you. You treat her with the same respect you would any of the old ladies."

I stare dumbfounded as Killian releases the guy and runs his eyes over each of his brothers. "She's important to me." He glances back at me and his expression softens. "I expect you all to treat her like family."

A wave of low murmurs fills the room as the guys offer their assent to their VP as I stand there with only one thought on my mind.

If my heart wasn't Killian's before...

It is now.

And I'm not sure I'll ever get it back.

22

CRANK

Killian: Wear a short skirt.

Sunshine: You trying to make me look like a club whore, Crank?

Killian: You're not the club's, you're mine. And who's Crank?

Sunshine: I'll see you soon. No pressure, but I've told Kat and Sadie that you've got something epic planned for our first date.

A groan rips from my lips. Of course she has. And she knows full well that if I fuck this up, I'll never hear the end of it.

Killian: I've got this, sunshine. Trust me.

Leaving my cut behind, I pocket my cell and make my way out of the cabin.

I dropped Quinn off late this morning so she could catch up with Sadie for lunch and I spent the whole time planning our date and cleaning the cabin.

It wasn't a mess, but it was more than obviously a bachelor's home. Now it's a home worthy of my girl. I know she's not going to get to spend all that much time here seeing as she's at school in Savage Falls, but I want to prove to her that I'm serious, that I'm not just saying the right thing, that I really mean those words about our future together.

Pulling my jacket on, I grab my keys and head out to where my bike's sitting out the front of the house.

I might have left my cut behind in the hope of showing Quinn that there's more to me than the MC, but there's no way I'm leaving my baby behind. I've got plans that involve her, after all.

The ride to the next town over is short, but I can't deny that there's a nervousness buzzing through my veins when I pull up outside Quinn's house.

I've never taken a girl out on a date before. I've never cared enough to want to spend time with them outside of the bedroom, so this is all new territory for me. I might be the oldest here, but right now, I may as well be the nervous high school kid about to spend his first night with the girl he's crushing on.

"Looking good, son," Micky says, pulling the door open and giving me the once over.

"She ready?"

The sound of footsteps on the stairs behind him hits me and my stomach knots.

"Sounds like it."

"Daddy," she sighs the second she sees him at the door. "Please don't give him the speech."

He looks at me and smiles, wicked intent glittering in his eyes.

"You're my baby girl, Quinn. I need to ensure that Crank knows just how strongly I feel about you remaining innocent until your wedding night."

Despite the fact I know he's joking, I swallow nervously.

He's shit out of luck when it comes to her having an innocent bone left in her body should we ever get as far as a wedding. I'll have dirtied her up beyond repair by this time next week, if I haven't already.

"Daddy," Quinn hisses before appearing over his shoulder.

The sight of her makes my breath catch.

Her hair is up, just a couple of strands hanging around her face. Like me, she's wearing a leather jacket but that's where the similarities end because beneath that is an emerald green dress that makes my mouth water.

"Holy shit,"

"Give me strength," Micky mutters, pushing back from the door. "For the love of God, just don't eat her alive."

"I promise to deliver her safely to school in the morning, Micky."

"Hmm... overnight—not exactly here before midnight, is it?"

"I'll make sure he treats me right, Daddy," Quinn assures him, dropping a kiss to his cheek.

"Come on, let's go before Mom has her say," she says to me, heading for the door.

"Sounds good. Night, Micky."

We're halfway across the driveway when he calls out to us. "My legs might not be working properly right now, Crank. But don't worry, I haven't forgotten how to use my gun."

"I got it, sir. She'll be treated like a princess."

"Oh my God, I'm going to kill him."

"He's just doing his job, sunshine. Let him have his fun."

"Mm-hmm," she hums as Micky shuts the front door, giving us some privacy.

"You look incredible," I say, letting my eyes linger on her now that we haven't got an audience. "And it's perfect for my plans." My eyes linger on the short hemline and her soft thighs beneath.

"Going to tell me where we're going yet?" she asks as I pass her a helmet.

"Nope. Hop on."

A sigh rips from my lips the second she wraps herself around me, her bare legs against my hips.

Gunning the engine, I take off fast, making her hold on tighter.

I take the long way to our destination, enjoying having her pressed up against me.

"What is this place?" she asks when I bring the bike to a stop, looking around at the deserted lot.

"The woods."

"And here I was thinking I got all dressed up for some fancy restaurant."

"Too cliché. You deserve something more... unique."

"Like you?" She asks, quirking a brow at me.

"Sure, just like that," I laugh. "Now, close your eyes."

"Umm..." she hesitates.

"Just do it, baby. I promise it'll be worth it."

Assuming she's done as she's told, I move forward through the trees until the date I set up comes into view.

Bringing the bike to a stop once more, I kill the engine. "You can look now."

I know the second she finds what I've done because her entire body tenses behind me.

"Killian," she breathes.

Unable to stand not seeing her reaction, I climb off my bike, leaving her on the back and turn toward her.

"You did all this?"

"I mean, I had a little help, but yeah. Do you like it?"

Her eyes hold mine, the flickering from the firepit reflecting back at me. "I love it, it's... you're incredible."

Dropping my eyes from her, I take her in wearing her tiny dress and sitting on the back of my bike. The black lace that covers her pussy teases me, but I push it aside for now. There will be time for that later. Tonight is about more than hearing her scream my name. It's about proving my worth.

"Come on, sunshine. Your date awaits."

I don't wait for her to climb off, I wrap my hands around her waist and lift her.

"Hey," she says, gazing up at me as I lower her to her feet.

"Hey. I missed you this afternoon."

"I was only gone for a few hours."

I shrug. "I'm a little addicted, sunshine."

Dipping my head, I capture her lips stealing a slow, passionate kiss from her.

"Mmm... I could get used to this," she says as I slip my hand into hers and guide her over to the blanket that's waiting for us.

The heat from the fire means it's warm enough for us to sit out and not get cold.

"I can't believe you did this. It's so romantic."

"I can do romance, sunshine. I just never wanted to before."

Opening the basket that's waiting for us, I pull out a bottle of bubbly and two glasses.

"Wow, you really have gone all out. Or is this just a plan to get me drunk?"

"Baby, I don't think I need alcohol to get between your legs these days."

Her cheeks flush and her eyes darken at my words. "You think I'm a sure thing, huh?"

Leaning over, I wrap my hand around the side of her neck. "I know it, sunshine. You want my mouth on your pussy as much as I do."

"Killian," she moans, her voice rough with arousal.

"Later," I promise, brushing my lips over her jaw and kissing down her neck.

"Or right now," she suggests temptingly, her fingers threading through my hair.

"Later," I growl with a chuckle. "I need to feed you first."

Putting some space between us, I pour us both a drink before grabbing all the food I brought.

We sit for hours chatting about everything as the sun makes its final descent in the sky and the stars begin to twinkle above it.

"This has been amazing," Quinn muses from her place tucked against my side as we lay staring at the night sky.

"Mmm," I mumble, kissing the top of her head. "I sure could get used to it."

Rolling into my side, her hand slips up my shirt as she props herself up on her elbow.

"Thank you."

"Just wanted to show you that I'm not always a sex addict biker."

Her eyes shoot to my crotch where my cock is pressing against the fabric of my pants. "Oh yeah?"

"You're touching me, sunshine."

"So I am." She drags her nails down my stomach and a growl rips up my throat.

Getting to her knees, she drops her lips to my ear. "I want to taste you," she whispers, her fingers expertly popping open my pants before slipping her hand into my boxers and grasping me.

"Baby," I moan as she strokes me in her firm grip.

"Pants, Kill."

I don't waste any time in pushing them down my hips, freeing my aching cock. "Fuck, sunshine," I moan when she licks the tip of me before sucking my entire length into her mouth. "Fuck, you're perfect. I love this. I love— Fuck."

She takes me all the way back cutting off any words that were about to fall from my lips.

I'm coming down her throat faster than I thought possible.

When she sits up, with her lips swollen from sucking me, I'm instantly hard again.

Will I ever get enough of her?

"My turn," I growl, dragging my pants back up and pushing to my feet.

"What are you—"

Scooping her up in my arms, I walk her toward my bike. "There's something I haven't been able to stop thinkin' about, sunshine. Wanna fulfill one of my fantasies?"

"I'll happily fulfill them all, Killi— Oh God," she moans when I lay her out along the length of the seat and spread her legs.

"Fuckin' perfect," I moan, running my eyes down the length of her body before zeroing in on her pussy. "You wet for me, sunshine?"

"Maybe you should find out." She rolls her hips, tempting me and my restraint snaps.

Tucking a finger under the soaked lace, I latch onto her clit, sucking hard and making her scream into the silence around us.

"That's it, baby. Nice and loud. I want the world to know who you belong to."

I've got a wide permanent smile playing on my lips as we walk into the clubhouse hand in hand after our date. I was happy to just take her home and continue what we started by the light of the fire, but Quinn was adamant that I don't have to give up club life because of her, and she knew via Kat that the guys were partying tonight, so she insisted we at least show our faces.

"River and Kat are over there. I'm gonna go hang," she says, reaching up on her tiptoes and pressing a kiss to the corner of my mouth.

"Okay. Be good."

"Pfft, as if I need a warning."

She squeals in shock as I slap her ass.

"Just make sure that no other motherfucker in here knows that your panties are currently in my pocket."

Desire floods her features.

"My pussy is all yours, caveman. I promise."

"Good." Just to make sure that everyone else in the room gets the message, I drag her into my body and slam my lips down on hers, kissing her until she's squirming and panting for me.

"You've got an hour, then I'm taking you home to keep you awake all night."

"Deal."

I watch her as she skips off toward her friends.

"Jesus," Diesel mutters when I sit on a stool next to his at the bar. "You are whipped as fuck."

"Meh, don't give a fuck, man. Cheers," I say when Tank passes me a beer before disappearing from behind the bar.

"It looks good on you." I study him for a beat, noting the dark shadows under his eyes.

"What's going on with you, man?" Guilt hitting

me for being so wrapped up in Quinn that I haven't noticed something is clearly wrong.

"It's nothing. It's just—" His words cut off as he looks over my shoulder, his brows pinching as he studies someone.

Following his stare, I look back to see who's captured his attention. He's looking right at the table where Quinn is sitting with Kat and... River.

No.

"Start talking," I demand, dragging his attention back to me.

"She kissed me," he confesses.

"And here I was thinkin' you'd adopted yourself a second sister."

He scoffs. "That's what I fucking thought."

"So what's the issue? She's single. Right?"

He rubs the back of his neck, regret shining bright in his eyes. "I pushed her away, told her it was a mistake."

"And it wasn't?" I ask, guessing where he's going with this.

"I don't fucking know, man. I just... I can't stop thinking about it. About her."

I can't help but laugh.

"Rhett is going to kill you."

Want more of the Red Ridge Sinners.
Download Ruin, book one in River's story now!

. . .

Meet Sadie, Rhett, Dane, and Wes in our RH, why choose romance, Savage Falls Sinners MC. Start the series with Savage.

Keep reading for a sneak peek!

SNEAK PEEK AT SAVAGE
CHAPTER 1

Sadie

"Sadie Ray, get your ass down here." My dad's gruff voice makes me bristle.

"I'm busy," I yell back, pulling a pillow from behind me and plastering it against my face.

"Don't make me come up there." A growl this time.

A growl that would have most people trembling with fear. But there isn't much about Raymond Dalton, prez of the Savage Falls Sinners MC, that scares me anymore. I've seen my dad broken and bloody, I've seen him almost choke a guy to death for looking at me wrong, and I've seen him shed tears for one of his lost brothers. He might be a giant of a man, all mean-looking tattoos, long dark hair, and menacing eyes, but nobody loves harder than Ray 'Razor' Dalton, despite what his club name might suggest.

The first thud of his boot against the stairs has me smirking.

The second has me shooting off the bed and darting for my small bathroom.

But before I can make the distance, he barrels into my room like a monster, heaving a deep breath.

"Seriously, Sadie," he grumbles, running a hand over his beard. "I asked you not to pull this shit." Something akin to pain flashes in his eyes, and my bravado slips for a second.

I'm being a brat, I know that, but he deserves it after what he's done—what he's about to do.

"What did you expect, Daddy?" I scowl, folding my arms over my chest for effect.

"Look, sweetheart, I know this isn't easy—"

"Easy? *Easy?*" I balk. "You're moving them in here and expect me to what? Play happy family? I didn't ask for this." I didn't ask for any of it.

He lets out a heavy sigh, tipping his face to the ceiling as if he's silently asking the universe to give him strength. I've seen him do that a lot in my life, as if he doesn't know what to do with me.

I guess sometimes he doesn't.

"I didn't ask for it either, Sadie, girl." He pins me with a pleading look. "But I made a promise to JD."

Guilt snakes through me. Thick and sludgy, it

fills me with shame... but then I remember what he did.

What he kept from me for all these years.

Before I can stop myself, I say, "Did JD also ask you to fuck his—"

"Don't," he seethes. "Don't talk about things you don't understand."

"Whatever, Dad." I barge around him and storm out of my room, flying down the stairs just as there's a knock.

My blood turns to ice as I glance back at my dad and force the most saccharine smile I can.

"Looks like my new brother and sister are here."

Dad moves around me, and it isn't lost on me that he's practically shielding me from them. But as he opens the door, it occurs to me that maybe he's shielding them from me.

My heart cinches as I drop down on the bottom step, waiting.

I've known for a while that Rhett and River Savage are moving in. They're my dad's best friend's kids. JD Savage. He died way back. Made my dad promise he'd always look out for them and their mom, but I guess that was one promise he couldn't keep.

Julia died a couple of weeks ago after OD'ing.

The whole MC attended her funeral, throwing a huge party after at the compound. If there's anything I've learned growing up as the club's princess, it's that bikers talk when they're drunk. But finding out that my dad planned to move Rhett and River into our house wasn't the only thing I overheard that day.

He'd loved her.

My old man had loved Julia Savage, his dead best friend's wife.

I've always known they were close, but I thought he was upholding a promise to a friend. I didn't think he was over in Colton, basically creating himself a new family.

I guess it explains a lot. Like why he's so close to Rhett.

Rhett Savage.

God, I hate that blue-eyed, tatted, cocky motherfucker. He's sin wrapped up in muscle and a dirty mouth... and now he's my what? Stepbrother?

The sting of betrayal sits heavy in my chest as I watch Dad welcome River into the house. She's everything I'm not. Slim and petite, with a waterfall of golden hair that falls over her shoulders. I'm all ass and boobs, and I take after my dad with my dark-as-night hair and dark green eyes.

River looks like Princess Barbie, standing there in her floral sundress and jeweled sandals.

"River, meet my daughter, Sadie Ray."

"Hey," she beams, and I flick my hand at her in a lackluster wave.

"Where's Rhett?" Dad cranes his neck to look around her.

"He's getting my things."

"Your things?" His eyes flash with irritation. "I'll go help him. You two girls play nice." He pins me with a warning look, and I narrow my eyes right back.

He ambushed me.

That bastard ambushed me, and I want to hate him for it... I do. But he's my dad. The one guy who's always been there for me, no matter what.

It's not that I resent him finding someone. I don't.

What I resent is him feeling the need to keep it from me.

"I love your hair." River moves closer.

My fingers drift to my wild curls, the flashes of bright pink highlighting them. "Thanks," I mumble.

"I'd never be brave enough to dye mine like that."

"So, you're River. I'm sorry about your mom." I didn't get to say that to her at the funeral, because I didn't realize her mom and my dad had been banging for years.

My chest tightens again.

"I've always wanted a sister." Something etches into her expression, but I'm too busy bristling at the word 'sister' to try to figure out what it is.

"That's... nice." I leap up and shove past her, heading down the hall to the kitchen.

I guess it's *our* kitchen now.

"Come on," I call over my shoulder. "I'll give you the tour."

River follows, gasping when she takes in our big, open-plan kitchen. It's by far the best room in the house. There's a huge oak table, big enough to seat ten burly bikers. It's the heart of the house, and my cousin Quinn and I have spent many a Sunday afternoon with my dad and aunt and our family—the Sinners MC—here. But that's not what catches River's eye. It's the wall of glass that overlooks the small lake.

"Wow," she moves closer, "it's so beautiful." Her eyes widen as she gazes outside, but the sadness never leaves them.

"Right?" I rest my elbows on the counter and watch her. She's not like I imagined, given that her big brother is Rhett Savage.

He's so... bad. And she's so... innocent. They couldn't be more different if they tried.

I don't know what to make of it.

He isn't exactly a talker, and he's always made it pretty clear he doesn't like me. Which is fine by me; the feeling is entirely mutual. It has absolutely

CAITLYN DARE

nothing to do with the fact that my dad treats him like the son he always wanted and never had.

Heavy footsteps in the hall draw both our attention, and Dad reappears. He eyes me warily, and I notice he's pulled his long hair into a ponytail. "We put your bags upstairs in your room."

"Thanks, Ray." River smiles, and it's so genuine, so full of gratitude, I want to wipe it right of her pretty little face.

Dammit.

She's like sunshine on a rainy day... and I feel like the thunderstorm circling overhead, about to erupt.

"Where's Rhett?" she asks.

"He's just getting the last of it. I'm surprised you talked him into borrowing a truck. I don't think I've ever seen that kid off his Street Bob."

"He doesn't let me ride his bike."

Of course he doesn't.

I fight the urge to roll my eyes.

"What do you think of the place?" Dad asks, and I swear he looks... nervous.

Razor Dalton doesn't get nervous. Ever.

This is fucked up.

"I love it. This kitchen is amazing. I—"

"I need to..." I thumb to the hall and inch back away from them both. This is too much too soon.

She's staring at Dad—*my* dad—likes he's her real-life hero, and he's acting weird.

I don't like it.

224

"Sadie Ray, wait—"

But I'm already out of the kitchen, darting down the hall. Anger burns through me as I grab the stair bannister and swing myself around... slamming straight into a wall of sheer muscle.

"Watch it, princess."

"Get out of my way," I grit out, lifting my chin at Rhett.

A slow smirk spreads over his face. "You ran into me."

"Whatever." I try to barge around him, but he plants his feet wider, crossing his ridiculously big arms over his chest. Even underneath his leather cut, I can see the way his white t-shirt molds to the hard lines of his chest.

"See something you like?"

"Please. I don't date bikers." My brow lifts in annoyance, but he only smirks harder.

"Who said anything about dating?"

Typical Rhett. He thinks he's God's gift to women. He might only be a year older than me, but he acts like he's something. Some*one*.

"Just stay out of my way," I hiss, my hands clenched into fists at my sides.

Amusement flashes in his eyes as he lets them drop lazily down my body, lingering on the low V-neck in my t-shirt.

"Gross. We're practically siblings, and you're looking at me like—"

"Rhett, that you?" Dad calls, his voice like a bucket of ice water over me.

I need to go. Now.

Using Rhett's momentary distraction to my advantage, I shove him—hard—and slip up the stairs, his deep rumble of laughter making my stomach knot.

Without looking back, I turn down the hall but pause when I hear Dad's voice.

"There's a room here for you, you know?"

"Yeah, I know."

"Stay. See how things go..."

"Nah. I like my space, and I have a room at the club."

"Yeah, but come on, son—"

Son. He called him son.

It shouldn't matter... and yet, I feel like I can't breathe.

"I appreciate it, Ray. We both do. But I'm not cut out for family life. Look after River. I'll stop by."

"Damn right you will. Go on," Dad says, "get out of here. I'll see you at the club later."

"Sure thing, old man."

Their laughter drifts up to me, making the knot in my stomach tighten. Rhett loves my dad, I know he does. It's in the way they talk: easy and fluid. It's the respect that shines in Rhett's eyes whenever my dad is around.

226

They're close.

Real close.

Which is why I've never understood why Rhett Savage acts like he hates me.

Download now to keep reading...

DELICIOUSLY DARK ROMANCE

Two angsty romance lovers writing dark heroes and the feisty girls who bring them to their knees.

SIGN UP NOW
To receive news of our releases straight to your inbox.

Want to hang out with us?
Come and join CAITLYN'S DAREDEVILS group on Facebook.

Ruin

Reap

Rule

Defy

Heirs of All Hallows'

Wicked Heinous Heirs - Prequel

Filthy Jealous Heir: Part one

Filthy Jealous Heir: Part two

Cruel Devious Heir: Part One

Cruel Devious Heir: Part Two

Brutal Callous Heir: Part One

Brutal Callous Heir: Part Two

Boxsets

Ace

Cole

Conner

Savage Falls Sinners MC